Cami Checketts

The Protective One: A Billionaire Bride Pact Romance
COPYRIGHT ©2016 by Camille Coats Checketts
All rights reserved

Birch River Publishing
Smithfield, Utah
Published in the United States of America
Cover design: Christina Dymock
Photo credits: LUTFI-LURE
Editing: Daniel Coleman

DEDICATION

To my twin sister, Abbie Anderson. Thanks for being my best friend and favorite sister. The research trip to Crested Butte was a hoot because of you. Now if I could just teach you how to flirt when men hit on you.

INTRODUCTION BY LUCY MCCONNELL

I've heard it said that some people come into your life and quickly leave—others leave footprints on your heart. Jeanette and Cami are two wonderful authors and women who have left their mark on my heart. Their overwhelming support, knowledge, and general goodness have pushed me forward as a writer and nurtured me as a friend. That's why I'm pleased to introduce you to their new and innovative series: The Billionaire Bride Pact Romances.

In each story, you'll find romance and character growth. I almost wrote personal growth—forgetting these are works of fiction—because the books we read become a part of us, their words stamped into our souls. As with any good book, I disappeared into the pages for a while and was able to walk sandy beaches, visit a glass blowing shop, and spend time with a group of women who had made a pact—a pact that influenced their lives, their loves, and their dreams.

I encourage you to put your feet up, grab a cup of something wonderful, and fall in love with a billionaire today.

Wishing you all the best,
Lucy McConnell
Author of *The Professional Bride*

THE BILLIONAIRE BRIDE PACT

I, MacKenzie Gunthrie, do solemnly swear that I will marry a billionaire and live happily ever after.

If I fail to meet my pledge, I will stand up at my wedding reception and sing the Camp Wallakee theme song.

CHAPTER ONE

MacKenzie Gunthrie flipped over on the hard bed in a large farmhouse somewhere in the Midwest. They hadn't told MacKenzie what state she was in, but there were definitely plenty of fields of corn and grain.

She massaged her left shoulder that had fallen asleep. She wished her entire body would fall asleep, but didn't hold out much hope. Sadly, she couldn't blame the uncomfortable bed for her insomnia. One week ago, MacKenzie witnessed torture and murder as she hid behind a trash can. In the wrong place at an absolutely horrific time. She shuddered. She'd never run at night again, and every time she closed her eyes all the images and panic-inducing terror came back. Sleeping was getting tougher and tougher.

Flinging onto her back, she squished around in the bed hoping to get comfortable but failed. A tear trickled out of the corner of her left eye and puddled in her ear. MacKenzie dug angrily at it. She muttered a quick, desperate prayer for help, not sure how much longer she could stand this uncertainty. She missed her parents, her sisters, her students, though school was out for the summer so she really couldn't see them anyway, and her friends and training partners. The quiet farm should've been preferable to the busy city of Chicago, but with at least two FBI agents by her side at all times and the fear always hanging over her, she didn't get any solitude. Miserable didn't begin to describe this night or the past week.

A gunshot rang through the farmhouse, followed by shouting. She jerked up in the bed. Her heart thudded against her rib cage. Sliding out from under the covers, she listened until the sound of more gunshots propelled her shaking legs into action. She dug her fingernails into her palms, trying not to remember the blood and the glint of the knife in the moonlight. Would the shock of having a finger completely cut off stem the pain at all? The high-pitched squealing and begging she couldn't ever get out of her mind told her no.

She slipped into a pair of Sanuks and pulled a T-shirt over her head just as her door sprang open. Agent Klein, a tall black man, who reminded her of her grandpa, gestured to her. MacKenzie was only a quarter African American. With her lighter skin and wavy dark hair, few people believed she and her grandpa were related, but she loved him and his heritage. Because of the similarities to Agent Klein, she had felt an instant connection.

"Let's go," Agent Klein barked.

MacKenzie followed him without question. She'd liked him from the first time they met, and instinct told her he was a person to trust. He took her arm and led her down the back staircase of the sprawling safe house and out into the dark summer night. The midnight blue sky was full of stars. MacKenzie liked the openness of this area and the smell of dirt and crops. So different than the busy streets of Chicago.

More gunshots rang out, seeming to ripple across the fields of corn, and she ducked.

"It's okay," Klein reassured her. "They're holding them off out front."

"Is it … Squirt?" MacKenzie squeaked out, barely able to vocalize the fears of who it might be.

"Yes." His face was as grim as his voice.

She and Klein had tried to joke about the situation she was in by calling Solomon Squire, Squirt. It hadn't lessened her fears by much, but it had helped. Squire's brother had been killed by the police when MacKenzie called 911 that fateful night. Solomon had escaped and MacKenzie was taken into protective custody until he was found. MacKenzie's own experiences with the man paled compared to the rumors she'd heard about the Chicago crime lord. He was bad news and no one tried to sugar coat that he would come after her in retribution for his brother's death.

They sprinted across the back yard and ducked into the barn.

Klein ushered her in, closed the door, and stood by it.

"We're just going to wait here?" MacKenzie's voice was a raw squeak.

"The other agents will take care of them then come get us with an all-clear."

"What if they don't ... take care of them?"

"Then I'll hold them off while you run. You like to run, right?" His white teeth flashed at her in the dimly lit barn.

MacKenzie's chest tightened. She loved to run, but the FBI agents hadn't let her out of the house by herself the past week, and because of how hard she'd trained the last six months to compete in national level Spartan obstacle races, none of them could keep up with her on a run. Her legs ached to run her favorite paved path in Chicago, sixteen miles along Lake Michigan. The sun on her face. Sweat pouring down her chest as she flew along the trail. Her only worry if she'd brought enough water to hydrate with.

"That's not funny, Klein," she muttered. "If they come, I'm not leaving you."

"Yes, you are. If it comes to that, you run and you run fast. I'll take care of them and then I'll find you. That pathetic Squirt isn't going to hurt you." He attempted a smile that she couldn't return, and finally settled for looking into her eyes until she meekly nodded.

She wished they could both jump in a vehicle and disappear, but everything was parked out front where the fight was concentrated.

Footsteps approached the barn. MacKenzie's pulse jumped.

"Hide in the back of the barn. There's a rear door if you need to use it." Klein gave her a gentle push. "Go."

MacKenzie scurried away and through the dim light found the rear door. She slowly slid it open and went outside, peeking back in to see what was going on. The front door of the barn creaked on rusty hinges as it swung wide.

"Klein?" a low voice called.

The air whooshed out of MacKenzie. It was Agent Tureen, not Squire or his men. Klein walked into the light from the open door.

MacKenzie waited for a signal from him.

"Where's the girl?" Tureen kept his gun pointed straight at Klein.

"She's gone," Klein said.

"Why?"

"I sent her to meet some agents coming from the north."

MacKenzie wondered why he would lie. The road ran north and south from the farm house, but if she ran from here, she'd be heading east.

Tureen cursed and pulled the trigger. Klein's body banged against the rough plank wall and slid to the ground. MacKenzie gasped then slapped a hand over her lips. Clutching her mouth with a trembling hand, she panted for air.

Tureen's head swung her direction. Luckily he was in the direct stream of light from the motion sensor outside the front of the barn. "MacKenzie? It's Agent Tureen. I'm here to protect you. Klein sold you out to Squire. We've contained the problem and you're safe now."

MacKenzie could hear gunshots out front. If they'd contained the problem, nobody should be shooting.

"It was all Klein." Tureen took a step into the barn. The door closed behind him.

MacKenzie didn't believe him. Whereas she'd trusted Klein, she'd never liked Tureen much. He seemed to be always checking her out or appraising her movements and comments in some way. His smooth voice reminded her of the crime lord, Squire—silky and deceptive.

Not waiting for his eyes to adjust to the darkness, she slid behind the rear door and slowly closed it. She ran as lightly as she could toward the cornfield. The uneven ground and rocks irritated her feet through the thin Sanuk's sole.

The back door of the barn banged open and Tureen rushed out. MacKenzie took the last few steps and was hidden among the corn. She slowed her pace, trying to minimize the noise as the green stems scratched at her arms. A bent-over stalk poked her in the face. She bit her lip so she wouldn't cry out and prayed the tall corn would hide

4

her.

Where was she going to go? Was it even possible to escape from him? Her stomach tumbled with fear and questions and her prayers became more desperate.

"MacKenzie?" Tureen called. "Come back now and things will go much better for you."

MacKenzie's throat was dry as she threaded through the corn. Tureen's voice grew fainter and when she couldn't hear him any longer, she thought it might be okay to run. She took Klein's advice, she ran fast and she didn't look back.

CHAPTER TWO

MacKenzie lifted several red, white, and blue decorative plates to the front of the display. The Fourth of July was only a couple weeks away and she wanted to make sure she sold these before she had to put them on discount.

She tilted her head to the side to study the arrangement and smiled.

"Excuse me, ma'am?"

MacKenzie's heart rate jumped at the voice behind her, but luckily she didn't physically leap. The past few days she'd improved at hiding her fears. That was *something* to be proud of.

She turned and smiled at the teenage girl. "Yes?"

"Can you help me find a birthday present for my granny?"

"Love to."

They searched the shop and settled on a Fourth of July wall hanging and red, white, and blue candles. MacKenzie waved goodbye to the girl and settled into the employee chair behind the desk.

Safe in the small valley of Crested Butte, Colorado she was thrilled to have a place to stay and a job. When she'd run that fateful night, she made it to a farmhouse several miles away. A sweet, old lady had hidden her in the back of her truck with her smelly pigs and driven for hours until there were no more police or agents searching for her. It had been the most miserable, terrifying night of her life, but the lady had believed her story and stayed with her until her parents wired her some money. She didn't dare go home, so she called one of the few numbers she had memorized, her old girl's camp friend, Haley Turnbow. Haley's number hadn't changed in years and it was an easy number to remember.

The timing was "perfect" in Haley's words for MacKenzie to come stay for a while. Haley was getting married and needed someone she trusted to run her home décor store, Sugar 'n Spice. MacKenzie didn't tell her friend the truth and she felt guilty about that, but Haley didn't need the kind of stress MacKenzie was dealing with when she was happily planning a wedding. Haley, her fiancée, Cal, and her five-year old son, Taz, had left shortly after MacKenzie arrived for Cal's island. They'd be back a couple days before the wedding.

It was a dream come true for MacKenzie. As long as she wasn't discovered in the picturesque mountain town, the Butte, as the locals called it. Her face pinched and her stomach turned at the thought of Agent Tureen or Solomon Squire finding her. She didn't know if she dared trust the FBI again, but had no clue who to trust if she couldn't trust them. If only Klein was okay. She didn't hold out much hope that he'd survived that shot. The only way she'd be safe to go home again was when she heard that Solomon Squire had been booked into a maximum security prison where he belonged. She sighed, hoping that day would come soon, but forcing herself to acknowledge it might never come.

"You keep pulling that face and it'll stick that way." The slow drawl of Haley's older brother, Isaac, from the open doorway made her stomach smolder, and that ticked her off almost as much as the insult, but at least she didn't jump in fear at a man's voice.

"Maybe I like my face this way." She stood to deal with him and wished his looks were as off-putting as his sarcastic personality. But no, his face was perfect—olive skin, manly lines, and those green eyes that drew her in. Of course he had to have dark hair with just the right amount of curl and beefy muscles in all the right places.

Isaac reached up and touched the skin next to her mouth. She tingled and tried to back away, but ran into the shelf. His hand dropped to his side.

"You look stressed."

"Thanks. Such a compliment."

"I'm sorry." He shoved a hand through his curls. "Haley would kick me in the pants if she knew you were unhappy. Take a break. I'll watch the shop for a while."

7

MacKenzie's eyebrows rose. "When did you decide to play nice?"

Isaac scowled. "You still mad at me because I called you one of the gold diggers?"

"Oh, big surprise that I would take offense to that." They'd met for the second time in over ten years the night she arrived in Crested Butte. The only downside of this escape plan was she'd been so excited to see Isaac again. He was her first—not to mention most amazing—kiss at the very mature age of fourteen. He hadn't remembered her or the kiss and that alone had about taken her under. His first line to her was, "Oh, another one of Haley's gold digger friends looking for a billionaire." What a jerk. A heartbreaking, much-too-good-looking jerk.

"Hey, I'm sorry, all right?" He glanced at the display over her shoulder. "Don't get all offended."

"Don't get all offended?" MacKenzie pushed around him, but unfortunately brushed against his muscular arm. She felt the connection all the way down to her toes and it frustrated her even more. Why was she always attracted to the Neanderthal idiots? If her body could pick a man to be attracted to who wasn't a sarcastic loser, she would be grateful. "I think I'll take that break, not sure if I'll make it back before closing time," she tossed over her shoulder.

Isaac nodded but didn't answer. She could feel his eyes on her as she left the store.

* * *

Isaac Turnbow pushed all his air out as he watched MacKenzie go. Crap. Apparently he'd said the wrong thing again. She was so breathtakingly beautiful it was like his mind got stuck because his eyes were too busy staring and he had no clue what he was saying until he realized that he'd upset her.

Isaac had finished feeding the calves early, got cleaned up, and told his dad he was going into town for a parts run.

"Make sure to check on MacKenzie," his dad had said with a huge smirk.

Isaac hadn't been able to hide his grin, knowing MacKenzie was the only reason he was coming to town. Now he'd messed up any chance of taking her to dinner tonight.

He strode to the front desk and plopped down on the employee's stool. Did she even remember their kiss? He'd been seventeen and much too full of himself, but she'd taken his breath away even then with her wavy brown hair framing naturally tan skin that was smooth and smelled intoxicating. Her lips were a perfect pink pout, even when she smiled, but his favorite part was her deep brown eyes filled with a mischievous sparkle.

They'd gone to a dance with Haley and some other friends. After a couple hours he'd convinced her to only dance with him and then he'd taken her down by the creek, away from all the noise and his sister's watchful eyes. The kiss had been more euphoric than hang gliding. He honestly couldn't say that another kiss had compared to it since. That definitely wasn't for lack of trying. He'd dated a lot of fun and interesting women in Crested Butte and when he went to University of Colorado, but he could never get MacKenzie's fine-boned features, sweet-tasting lips, and easy way of bantering with him, out of his mind. She'd changed in the past ten years. More beautiful, but there was something in her eyes now, the innocence was replaced by a wariness that made him wonder if something traumatic had happened to her.

The door swung open and Isaac's fists immediately clenched. Brad Hall strode in confidently, but faltered when he saw Isaac sitting at the counter. "Oh, um." He backed toward the door. "What happened to the hot girl working here this morning?"

Isaac stood and folded his arms across his chest. "That *hot* girl is my fiancée and I'd appreciate you never looking at or talking to her. We clear?"

Brad nodded quickly, though his eyes betrayed that the weasel would be all over MacKenzie, given any sort of chance, even if he did think she was engaged. Isaac hated the entire crooked Hall family, especially Brad. He never wanted to think about the fact that Brad was Isaac's nephew's biological father. Taz had a real father now in Haley's fiancé, Cal Johnson, and if Brad even glanced in Haley's direction Isaac wouldn't have to kill him—Cal would do it for him.

He blamed himself all the same for the damage Brad had inflicted on Haley. He should've pummeled Brad repeatedly years ago. Haley still didn't know about the one time he had thumped Brad, but it had accomplished the goal—Brad promised never to touch Haley again. If the police chief had given Isaac grief for months, such as tickets for going a mile over the speed limit, well that was one of the hazards of living in a small town that was firmly in the Hall's back pockets.

Brad hurried to the door and swung it open. "See ya," he mumbled on his way out.

Isaac didn't respond. He growled and paced the small lobby of the store. Luckily there were no customers to see his agitation. What if Brad ran into MacKenzie? He would smooth talk her and do anything he could to worm his way into her good graces. The thought made Isaac want to rush out and find her so he could protect her. He thought about MacKenzie's quick retorts and smiled. Maybe she'd tell Brad off before he got a chance to manipulate his way into her heart.

Hopefully Brad would believe they were engaged. Isaac stopped pacing. His heart thudded loudly in his chest. He'd told Brad they were engaged. It was only to protect MacKenzie, but what if she found out? She would not like that, not one bit. Oh, no. Flipping the switch so the open sign dimmed, Isaac wrote a hurried note, *Be back in 15*, shoved it in the window and locked the door behind him. He needed to find MacKenzie before Brad did.

CHAPTER THREE

MacKenzie stormed down Elk Avenue, the main street in Crested Butte, dodging tourists and locals out enjoying the mild summer day. Bikes and cars leisurely shared the narrow road. She muttered, "Excuse me," as she sped around a family with two little boys and three huge dogs. She didn't want to be rude, but all she cared about at the moment was escaping from that infuriating man.

How dare Isaac call her a gold digger? Just because her and her friends had made a silly pact at girl's camp to marry rich men when they were too young to even understand how fickle and frustrating men were. A few of her friends had married billionaires, but they'd done it because they loved them. Isaac's sister, Haley, was marrying Cal in a couple of weeks and he was filthy rich, but such a cool, down-to-earth guy. Why did Isaac make her feel like she needed to defend her friends, their husbands, and especially, herself? Ooh, he made her boiling mad.

Third Bowl Homemade Ice Cream appeared at her right. If that wasn't divine intervention, she didn't know what was. She only had a few dollars to her name until she got paid next week, but there was plenty of food at the house she was staying at and ice cream was worth spending her last bit of cash on. Especially when she needed chocolate to calm her nerves, since she couldn't setup a life-size poster of Isaac Turnbow and throw spears at it. Oh, that would be happiness. She ruled the spears at Spartan competitions.

She went through the open door and climbed the stairs to the ice cream shop. The walls were painted bright turquoise blue and orange and a huge blackboard hanging behind the ice cream cases listed all the flavors. Pictures of adorable babies and children eating ice cream competed for every bit of free space on the walls. The smell of sweet cream made her smile and that was a very welcome thing.

11

A cute teenage girl with glasses and blonde hair grinned at her. "Hi! What can I getcha?"

"Um, what's your specialty?"

The girl gestured to the blackboard. "They're all amazing! I come in on my days off just to try a different kind. Then I plop down with a romance novel and you could just pluck and stuff me because I'm already in heaven."

MacKenzie smiled. Ice cream, romance lover, and a bit of spunk. This girl was a kindred spirit. "What's your favorite?"

"Hmm. Today?" She pursed her lips. "Raspberry goat cheese or coconut stout chip."

MacKenzie wrinkled her nose at the thought of goat cheese in ice cream. She did like coconut, but not nearly as much as chocolate.

"Do you want to try a sample?"

"Thanks, I'll look them over and let you know." MacKenzie perused the board that included some really odd flavors like cranberry crumble, green chile chocolate, rosemary honey pecan, and blood orange dark chocolate. She needed chocolate, but she wasn't ready to try anything crazy. She ordered a child's scoop of the regular dark chocolate on a sugar cone. The girl was dishing it up and chattering about how much she loved Lucy McConnell's romances. MacKenzie promised to buy one on her Kindle, not wanting to think about the fact her Kindle was in her apartment in Chicago and she may never get back to it.

Another customer ascended the stairs and the girl stopped talking and focused on the ice cream. The man looked familiar. MacKenzie thought he may have been in Haley's store yesterday. The man was tall, almost as tall as Isaac, but not as broad. He had dark hair and eyes and an extremely handsome face, more of a model kind of face where Isaac's was more of a manly good look. She rolled her eyes at herself. Why was she comparing anyone to Isaac? That was giving the jerk much more brain time than he deserved.

The man smiled at her and called to the girl. "Charlie, give me a double rosemary honey pecan in a bowl with hot fudge, and I've got hers." He winked at MacKenzie and handed over ten dollars before MacKenzie could react.

Charlie lifted the ice cream cone over the top of the freezer to MacKenzie, took the money, and got busy scooping the man's ice cream. Her darling smile had disappeared and she said nothing.

MacKenzie glanced at the man, who was blatantly checking her out. His eyes went down and up enough times she wanted to ask him if he had an optical disorder.

"Thank you," she murmured instead. "You didn't need to do that." She took one lick of the ice cream and was grateful the man had paid. Now she had five dollars left to come buy ice cream again before she got her check.

"Sure, I did." He leaned against the freezer and pumped his eyebrows. "Prettiest girl I've ever seen comes to town, the least I can do is buy her ice cream to thank her for coming."

MacKenzie had to laugh at his attempt at being smooth. "Must be a lame town if I'm the prettiest girl to ever come here." She was confident enough in her looks, but she knew there were some men who weren't interested in a girl with a burly, redheaded Irish dad and a rail thin Polynesian-African-American mom. It used to bother her a lot as a teenager that she had a mixed background, but now she loved it and was proud that her family didn't see color. Maybe that was why Isaac was so off with her. He looked like some kind of Roman royal with his dark hair, green eyes, and olive skin. Probably thought he was superior. The thought made her like him even less.

"Not lame at all. I can show you around if you'd like." The man licked his lips.

"Maybe some other time." She walked around him. "Thanks again for the ice cream." Descending the stairs, she found a bench out front and sat down. It was a beautiful summer afternoon. The temperatures here were so much milder than the steamy warmth of Chicago in the summer. The high today probably wouldn't reach eighty. Isaac had told her to take a break. She was going to heed his advice and hopefully by the time she got back she'd be ready to play nice with her employer's brother.

Across the street in front of the restaurant, Bonez, there was a large group of people in suits and dresses. Most people walked around Crested Butte in biking or hiking gear so it was strange to see people dressed so fancy. MacKenzie heard cheers erupt and turned to see a bicycle procession coming slowly down the street. A handsome young man in a tux rode the front seat of a tandem bike with his gorgeous bride perched on the back. About twenty other people in suits and formal dresses rode on bikes behind the couple. The parents were obvious on their own tandem bikes with proud, happy looks and tears streaming down their faces.

"Oh, she is lovely," an elderly lady said next to MacKenzie. "Grew up right here in Crested Butte then went away for college. I taught her ballet when she was seven."

MacKenzie smiled, watching the couple glide past. "She is a beauty."

"Why do they have to grow up so fast?" The lady dabbed at her eyes then walked across to Bonez.

MacKenzie wondered if this was a tradition for Crested Butte locals, riding their bikes down Elk Street to celebrate their marriage with the town. She wondered if Isaac would be riding on a tandem bike someday with his bride behind him. The thought turned her stomach and her ice cream lost its flavor.

The man who'd paid for her ice cream plopped down on the bench next to her. "Do I get to meet the girl I just bought ice cream for?"

"Three dollar ice cream cone?" MacKenzie scooted a few inches away and forced Isaac and images of what his bride might be like from her brain. She took another lick of frozen heaven and tilted her head to the side. "Not sure that's going to get you a meet and greet."

He laughed. "How about if I bought you dinner tonight?"

MacKenzie shook her head. "Dinner might get you a handshake, but I'm not available tonight."

"It's true then."

"What's true?"

"You're engaged to that idiot, Isaac Turnbow."

"*What?*" MacKenzie dropped her ice cream cone. It splatted softly on the concrete, but she hardly noticed. *Engaged to Isaac?* Her stomach started a low burn and her breath shortened. What if *she* was the girl on the back of his tandem bike? Would she cling to his trim waist or his strong shoulders? Would she lean into him and savor each touch and smell, or be too busy waving to loved ones from the back of the bike, and sharing the joy of their day?

No! She had to stop before she kept right on imagining things like a shared kiss over the altar and beyond.

"MacKenzie," a deep voice called out, uncertain and manly, and if she hadn't been so upset and confused, she might've liked the sound of that voice calling out her name.

She glanced up and met the green eyes of the very man in question, storming up the sidewalk toward them.

Jumping to her feet, she faced him. "You told him I'm engaged to *you?*" her voice came out all shrill like a witch on a warpath.

Isaac's face blanched, but he didn't slow his stride.

The other man stood to the side of her, but backed away. "Isaac, I didn't … it was just, ice cream."

Isaac slammed his fist into the man's face. The guy's head flew back and his feet shot out from under him. He fell ungracefully to the concrete. MacKenzie gasped, wringing her hands together.

Isaac stood over him, his voice low and threatening. "Don't you ever come near her again or so help me, I'll make you wish you were dead."

The oxygen rushed from her body. MacKenzie dropped to her knees next to this poor man who had done nothing but buy her ice cream. Blood trickled down the man's split lip. MacKenzie gagged, all the memories rushing back. Her hands trembled, but she wouldn't back down. She hadn't been able to save that man from Solomon Squire but she could stand up to Isaac.

He took a step closer and her spine stiffened. "You had better back up," she said through clenched teeth.

"Please, MacKenzie, let me explain." Isaac held up his hands innocently. His eyes filled with concern.

"Don't you talk to me!" Her body was shaking. She clenched her hands to try to regain control and focused on the man, whose nose was swelling. There were some napkins from her ice cream cone on the concrete. She grabbed the cleanest one and dabbed away the blood on his mouth.

"I'm so sorry," she murmured. "I have no clue why he would claim we're engaged or why he would hit you for no reason." Why did she have to keep being involved in violence? She couldn't handle much more.

"There's a reason, believe me." Isaac blew out a long breath. "Please, MacKenzie."

"That's just the way he is," the man said.

"I'm so sorry he hit you."

"You don't have to be sorry." He smiled an awkward, sad smile.

MacKenzie felt relieved he wasn't blaming her. She could not believe Isaac's cave man attitude. "I'm MacKenzie Howe." The lie slipped out easily and she hoped Maryn wouldn't mind her stealing her maiden name for a little while. "What's your name?" she asked the man.

"Brad." He pushed his way to his feet and MacKenzie stood with him.

She turned her back on Isaac, grabbed Brad's hand, and urged him to walk with her. "Is your nose okay?"

Brad threw a dark look over his shoulder. "It'll be fine. It's not the first time he's hit me."

"Oh, my, heck!" MacKenzie also glared back at Isaac. He watched the two of them with a mixture of frustration and helplessness on his face. How could her darling friend Haley have a brother who was a brawling caveman? MacKenzie had fancied herself in love with him as a teenager and minutes ago she'd daydreamed about riding on the back of his tandem bike. Her face heated with shame. At least she knew what he was like now. "I'd love to go to dinner with you," she

16

told Brad.

Brad grinned and seemed to forget about his red nose, cut lip, and swollen cheek. He wrapped his arm around her waist. "What do you feel like, Mexican, Italian, home-cooking? We've got some of the greatest restaurants in Crested Butte."

MacKenzie stiffened at his casual touch. In life before protective custody, she'd been preparing to be on an elite Spartan team that was hoping to compete in the intense obstacle race at a national level. One of her male teammates, Vince, was always overly familiar, touching her and hugging her. Brad reminded her of him. She knew it was innocent, but she just wasn't a casual romance kind of girl. She wanted a marriage like her parents—committed, loving, and comfortable.

"Italian sounds great."

"Perfect."

MacKenzie glanced over her shoulder once more. Isaac watched them through hooded eyes. His fists clenched tightly at his side. He met her gaze and mouthed, "Please."

MacKenzie whipped her head back around. Her throat so dry she couldn't swallow. What right did Isaac have to ask her please anything? He'd just punched a man for no reason and he'd made her drop a perfectly delicious ice cream cone.

Regardless of Isaac's feelings on the matter, she wasn't ready to cozy up to another man she didn't know. She stepped away from Brad and his arm dropped to his side. He gave her an injured look, but didn't say anything.

They walked past Haley's store and she saw the scribbled sign, *Be back in 15*. At least it looked like Isaac had locked up. Should she be going to dinner and leave the store unattended? She forced herself not to care. Isaac could take care of the store. He deserved some extra work for his treatment of Brad.

She and Brad walked a block east on Elk Avenue then around the corner to a clapboard building, *Marchitelli's Gourmet Noodle* hung from a small sign. Most of the restaurants in town were either open for breakfast and lunch, or didn't open until after five. This one must be the latter as it was barely five.

A smiling hostess dressed all in black seated them. Satiny white fabric hung from the ceiling and covered the tables and windows. For some reason it reminded MacKenzie of the inside of a coffin. The ceilings were high enough she didn't feel claustrophobic, but the thought of a coffin brought her back to Solomon Squire and the death knoll following her. She took a steadying breath and tried to push those fears away.

Brad told the waitress to bring them an order of stuffed mushrooms and a bottle of cabernet.

"I'll just have water, please," MacKenzie said, trying to relax in the black vinyl seat, but not feeling completely comfortable with this guy. She'd wanted to protect him when he'd gotten hurt, but had gone with him afterward mostly to tick Isaac off. Now she was questioning her decision. Trusting someone unknown didn't used to be this scary. Curse Solomon Squire for disturbing every part of her life.

Brad frowned, but his smile was quick to return. "Not a drinker?"

"Not really." As an elite athlete she didn't usually drink and now she wanted to be in control all the time in case Squire found her and she had to disappear quickly.

"Where are you from?" Brad asked.

"California," MacKenzie was quick to lie. She'd decided to use a story similar to her friend, Maryn, for her background. It made it easier to lie when the story was familiar. She knew hiding from the FBI wasn't smart, but she didn't know if Tureen had been the only agent that had sold out to Squire. She felt safer in this out of the way valley than in FBI custody until Squire was caught. She checked online every night to see if that miracle had happened and she could go home.

"Are you and Haley … close friends?" Brad studied her carefully.

"We went to girl's camp together, but haven't been as close as adults. Keep up on Facebook and Friend Zone. I was excited to come help her before the wedding," she added hastily lest he think it odd that she was here visiting if they weren't close friends.

Brad reclined into his chair. "Well, I hope you and I can be *close* friends."

His fingers brushed over hers. Haley pulled back and gave him a stiff smile. Thankfully, the waitress returned with the spectacular-looking mushrooms and a basket of crusty bread with herb butter. One bite of the rich, buttery appetizer, she was almost glad Isaac had hit Brad and convinced her to go to dinner with the man. Plus, now she knew exactly what Isaac was like. She'd stay far away from him.

CHAPTER FOUR

Isaac banged his way into his fifth-wheel trailer. The short drive from town to the ranch and working for an hour on his metal work art hadn't calmed him. All he'd done was make a mess of some custom orders. He finally quit work and tried to find something decent for dinner in his small fridge.

He hated Brad Hall with every ounce of his body. Now Isaac had made himself look like an out-of-control jerk in front of MacKenzie and she was going to fall for Brad's tricks. He couldn't allow that to happen, and not just because he wanted to be the one taking her to dinner. He wouldn't let another woman he cared about be taken advantage of by that loser.

A loud knock reverberated throughout the trailer. Isaac glanced out his window and sighed when he saw the cop car. "Just my luck."

He swung the door open and nodded to his friend, Joshua. "Captain Crusie."

Josh held out a ticket, his brown eyes sober. "Why'd you hit him this time?"

Isaac took the ticket and grimaced. Five-hundred dollars. That was going to dip into his savings for his land and shop. Land was just too expensive in Crested Butte now. Maybe he should focus on buying in Gunnison instead. That would really tick his dad off.

He pushed a hand through his hair. It needed a cut, the curls were getting out of control. "He hit on my sister's friend."

Josh nodded. "The girl working at Sugar 'n Spice?"

"Yeah."

"I'll watch out for her."

"That's what I was trying to do." Something flared in him. A primal instinct of protection and desire. *He* needed to be the one watching out for MacKenzie. If he could just convince her he was the good guy here, maybe she would trust him and learn to like him.

"I know, but you get fines when you try to watch out for women." He pointed to the ticket in Isaac's hand and shook his head. "Change is happening, bro, but it's not going to be fast."

Isaac arched an eyebrow. "You're willing to risk your job to help this town escape the oppression of the Hall family?"

Josh elevated his shoulders. "I'm doing what I can. The Sheriff is up for election this year and they've talked Mason into running."

"He's a good man."

"Most of the police department isn't bowing to the Hall's demands anymore and your brother-in-law buying One Hill Resort and dumping money into some businesses is helping as well. They realize with all the new money coming in, we don't have to rely on the Halls for financial support in this town."

His future brother-in-law, Cal, was a great guy and had taken an interest in the town for Haley's sake, but unfortunately hadn't run Brad and his dad out of business or politics yet. Most of the new money in the valley cared little about local politics since they were buying property for second or third homes. They didn't care who ran the town as long as the snow was good for skiing.

"I hope you're right, but why am I the one getting a ticket?" *While the scumbag is at dinner with the beautiful lady?* He restrained himself from asking that as he held up the piece of paper.

"You can't just haul off and punch somebody, especially when it isn't the first time you've done it."

Isaac's shoulders rounded. He needed to control his temper, which oddly only manifested itself when Brad showed up. Yet he wasn't going to allow Brad to hurt MacKenzie the way he'd hurt his sister, Haley.

"I talked Sheriff Ono out of jail time and down to the lower fine."

Isaac shook his friend's hand. "Thanks."

"How's the welding art coming?"

Isaac smiled. "Good, I've got a lot of special orders and have sold out of almost everything online and at Haley's store. I just need time to work more and to be able to invest in marketing, plus a place of my own."

"Why don't you just have your brother-in-law spot you some money?"

"A man's got to have some pride." No way was he begging Cal and Haley for money so he could succeed at his dreams and find his independence in the process. He'd keep working hard and dreaming reasonable and someday he'd be a success and prove to this town and his father that he wasn't just a ranch hand.

"There's a limit to the amount of pride one man needs." Josh chuckled and walked away.

Isaac watched him go then set the ticket on the counter and went to his shop. Dinner would have to wait. Maybe he could work away the worry that Brad was going to hurt MacKenzie. She'd made it more than obvious she didn't want Isaac's help, but what could he do to protect her? He dialed Haley's number. If anyone could warn MacKenzie away from that loser, Haley could.

* * *

MacKenzie pulled into the driveway of Haley's house in the beat up car she'd found some farmer selling on the edge of his property. The car had been a steal at five hundred dollars, and had survived the thirteen-hundred mile drive from Ohio to Colorado.

Dinner with Brad had turned out to be fun, though it had lasted a lot longer than she would've liked. She was more than ready to put up her feet and relax with one of the latest football romance novels by Taylor Hart she'd seen on Haley's bookshelf.

Haley's house was a darling cottage-style, decorated to the hilt, not surprising considering Haley owned a home décor store. MacKenzie liked things clean and orderly, which was a struggle as a school teacher of adorable but rowdy second graders. She sometimes wondered if she had sensory overload and the disorder was getting worse as she watched over her shoulder for Squire and prayed no one was tracking her. She wouldn't have minded more sparse decorations, but wasn't going to mess with anything in the house. Haley's generosity was literally saving her life.

She opened the door of the 1998 Accord, wincing at the squeak. She'd have to buy some WD40 and hope that would fix it. She wasn't bad with the basics under the hood. After raising three girls in Lake Forest, a northern suburb of Chicago, her dad decided the youngest should at least know how to change a tire and her oil. She missed her parents and older sisters and wished she dared contact them, they were probably going nuts worrying, but that would be one of the first places that Solomon Squire would look.

She didn't hold out a lot of hope that Squire would be arrested soon. The FBI had been trying to capture him and his brother for years. They were slippery, ruthless, well-connected, and wealthy. Horrible combination for criminals.

Trudging her way to the front porch, she spied a shadow next to Isaac's shop. A scream escaped before she could rein it in and she cursed herself for alerting the person to her position. No, no, no!

MacKenzie spun and doubled back to the car at a full sprint. Briefly, she wondered if she should run to Isaac's trailer or Haley's dad, Trevor's, rambler. Haley's house was right between the two, but escaping alone was smarter than putting anyone else in danger. But even if she could escape, where would she go now? Despair overwhelmed her.

She gasped for air, her limbs prickling from terror. The image of being tortured then killed like the man she'd seen die was suffocating. A hand wrapped around her arm and she didn't hold back the scream this time, "Help! Please, somebody help!" she gasped out. It was wrong to involve Haley's family in her nightmare, but Isaac seemed more than capable and strong, and in her fear she just wanted someone to help.

The man tried to drag her to a stop, but she kept plowing toward her car in desperation, straining to break his grip. The car was feet away.

"MacKenzie. It's me. I'm not going to hurt you." Isaac's voice penetrated through her fear.

She stopped struggling and glanced up into his vibrant green eyes. "Isaac?" she whimpered. Before she knew what she was doing, she'd flung herself against his chest. "Oh, thank heavens. Oh, thank you, Lord." She closed her eyes and repeated prayers of gratitude out loud and internally.

When she calmed down a little bit and stopped praying, she realized Isaac's brawny arms had encircled her and her cheek was pressed against his bulging chest muscles. He smelled like metal, musk, and man. Oh, yum. Her heart began to race from a completely different reason than fear. It took almost a full minute for her to gain control enough to pull away out of sheer embarrassment. This was Isaac. Haley's annoying older brother who didn't even remember he was her first kiss.

Her eyes narrowed as she stared him down or rather up. "How, why, I mean, *what* were you thinking?"

His brow wrinkled. "I'm sorry I chased you, I didn't mean to scare you, but wow, MacKenzie, what is going on? I've never seen someone that scared before."

MacKenzie's face flared. She couldn't tell him why she was scared and luckily the righteous indignation gave her the fuel she needed. "I'm not talking about *that*. I'm talking about how you dared to tell Brad that we're engaged!" She folded her arms across her chest. Better to redirect than tell him why she was running.

Of course, the cocky jerk didn't back away or even look embarrassed. He moved closer into her personal space. "Brad Hall is bad news. I can't allow you near him."

"Can't allow?" She gave a sarcastic laugh. "You have no right to tell me who to be near or to punch someone because I might like them."

"You don't, do you?" Isaac's handsome features twisted in concern.

"Don't what?" She gritted her teeth and then arched her eyebrows

24

at him.

"*Like* him," Isaac roared.

MacKenzie was tall, but Isaac had her by half a foot. She arched her head back, refusing to step away and give him the satisfaction that he intimidated her. Somehow she knew he would never hurt her, but she didn't appreciate being talked down to like this. And why did she keep getting whiffs of his manly scent and noticing how nicely his biceps were formed? Ooh, that made her almost as mad at herself as she was at him.

"Maybe I do like him," she taunted. It would serve the big oaf right if she felt something that he obviously didn't want her to feel. This wasn't about Brad at all. It was about putting Isaac in his place.

"No." Isaac exhaled loudly. "You can't. Please, listen to me." He wrapped both hands around her upper arms. It wasn't enough pressure to hurt her or keep her from moving out of his grip, but the warmth of those large hands seared through her and her stomach took flight. "Brad is a manipulative liar. If you don't believe me, ask Haley. Did she call you?"

MacKenzie was disgusted at her body's natural reaction to this man. It was all she could do to keep from leaning into him again.

She'd turned her phone to silent after Haley had tried to call her twice during dessert. "It's none of your business if I date Brad, or if Haley calls me, and I'll thank you to never tell someone that you and I are engaged. We aren't even friends for heaven's sake."

Isaac's entire body stilled. He simply stared at her with those too-green eyes and Haley swayed under his spell. Those eyes must be like snake eyes that could charm a woman and make her obey his every command. His hands gently rubbed up and down her arms and his voice went low and soft, "I wish we were friends, MacKenzie. You don't know how I've wished for that."

MacKenzie was spellbound by his look and the soft touch of his hands for a few delicious seconds. "But, we-we're, um, not friends," she whispered, stuttering all over herself.

"I think you'd like being friends with me." Isaac bent closer. His eyes flickered down to her lips before returning to her eyes and his warm hands worked their way up her arms across her shoulders and down to her back, making her tremble. He gently pulled her in. Any fear or worry she'd had evaporated. His touch brought safety, excitement, and heady desire.

"Uh … what?" MacKenzie's mind had turned to mush while her body had turned to fire. What was he *doing* to her?

"Friends?" He lowered his head until his mouth was inches away.

MacKenzie's heart slammed against her chest. She panted for air. He grinned slightly then his lips touched hers and everything in her calmed as if Isaac was where she should be centered and he was the person who could protect and love her. Then her body responded and she went on tiptoes, wrapping her arms around his neck. The kiss became electric. Her heart took off at a sprint and every nerve seemed to tingle with happy receptors working overtime.

Isaac's hands worked their way around to frame her face while she clung to his muscular back. A small moan escaped her. He tilted her face and took his time slowing down the kiss and wiping all rational thought from her mind.

Isaac broke the kiss and rested his forehead against hers. "I think I'm going to like being friends with you." He gave her that cocky grin that drew her in and infuriated her at the same time.

MacKenzie's chest heaved. She'd almost forgotten a kiss could be so invigorating, all-encompassing, heavenly. But no. This was Isaac. Infuriating, too-confident Isaac. She didn't like him or the way he treated her. First, claiming she and her friends were gold diggers then lying about being engaged and punching people.

Snapped back to a cold, dreary reality, she pulled away and his hands dropped from her face. "No, you're not, because we aren't friends and we definitely are not engaged."

His grin disappeared and she wished she could restore it, but that was wrong. He couldn't just kiss her and claim they were friends. Besides, she didn't go around kissing her friends, especially not like that. She touched a hand to her lips and depression set in at the thought of never experiencing Isaac's kiss again.

"And, and …" She tried to conjure up a threat to keep him from looking at her like a wounded puppy. "And I'm going to tell Haley exactly how big of a jerk you were tonight." She stomped around him, face flaming at her immature words. Maybe being back here again was making her act like her fourteen year old self. She rushed up the porch steps, slamming the door on the way into her house.

She dead-bolted the door and leaned against it for support. Heaven help her, she was attracted to Isaac. He wanted her to be friends. Friends with benefits she couldn't allow herself to indulge in daydreaming about. Oh, my. She should've been stronger. How could she have let him kiss her? She'd have to be more careful and stay far away from him. Brad Hall was safe. Isaac Turnbow was… No, no, no! He was a whole bucket full of no for her.

MacKenzie checked every window and double-checked the deadbolts on the front and back doors before changing into some comfy sweats, locking herself in her bedroom, and checking the phone Haley had given her as part of the business arrangement. Haley had been so caught up in pre-marital bliss she hadn't even asked where MacKenzie's phone had disappeared to.

She'd missed ten calls and seven texts from Haley. Instead of listening to the four voice mail messages she hit the callback button.

"Oh, Kenzie, thank heavens. Please don't tell me you were alone with Brad."

"It was just dinner at Marchetelli's. Did Isaac tell you he punched him?"

"Good!" The vehemence in sweet Haley's voice shocked her. "I wish he could do worse than that to Brad."

"Whoa, wait a minute. Isaac is the one at fault here. He claimed that he and I were engaged." *Then he kissed the dickens out of me.* That moment was not getting shared. At least not by her. She wondered if Isaac would tell Haley about their interactions today. Had the kiss affected him at all? Would *he* share it?

"He did?" Haley whistled. "Isn't he a sweetie? He was trying to protect you from Brad. Unless, maybe he had ulterior motives. I remember you two liking each other when you came to visit."

"Ten years ago! We *definitely* don't like each other now." Liked kissing each other, but that didn't count.

"Oh." Haley's voice fell. "That's a bummer. No matter what, though, stay away from Brad."

"Why?"

"He's Taz's father, Kenz."

"Oh, my." MacKenzie didn't know the whole story, but she knew Haley hated Taz's father.

"He drugged and raped me."

"Wait. Wh-what?"

"Yeah," Haley whispered. "You heard right." She paused and MacKenzie had no clue how to respond. Poor Haley.

"I'm ... so sorry."

Haley cleared her throat. "Isaac and my dad have wanted Brad to serve time or do their own renegade justice, but the police chief in our town was being paid off by Brad's dad so nobody could do anything."

MacKenzie's stomach was rolling. She'd escaped from Solomon Squire and put herself in a situation that could've been almost as awful. Rape. It was such a horrifying word. "I'm really sorry, Haley. He seemed charming," she muttered.

"I bet he did," Haley's voice was full of bitterness. "Can you please promise me to stay away from him?"

MacKenzie nodded, even though Haley couldn't see it. "Of course I will. Thanks for all you're doing for me."

"It's helping me out tons." Haley exhaled as if relieved to be done with that part of the conversation. "We'll be back in town Saturday to finish the final prep for the wedding on Thursday. Isaac was giving me a hard time about getting married in the mountains when I could have a destination wedding here on Cal's island, but I think we'll have less chance of paparazzi in Crested Butte. A lot of our friends have problems with that now."

MacKenzie's face scrunched up. Isaac. He seemed destined to

give everyone a hard time. "You should do what *you* want."

"I am, don't worry. Cal spoils me far too much."

MacKe nzie smiled. Her friend was so happy and in love. She was thrilled for Haley, but knew such a happy ending could never happen in her own life, at least not until Squire was arrested and she somehow got back to her own reality. Yet there'd be no Isaac in Chicago to infuriate and excite her. She shook her head and focused on what Haley was saying about wedding plans. Isaac didn't deserve a spot in her desires.

CHAPTER FIVE

Isaac slammed a hay bale into the trough. Cutting the strings off, he pushed it out to the cows. Usually when he worked, his mind would conjure all kinds of ideas for welding projects. Everything from the horses in the next stall over and the towering mountains and cascading pines gave him ideas for something to weld. He'd started to sell his work online and it was going well. Because of Haley's insistence that he upped his prices, most of his pieces sold for thousands of dollars. If he could just get his own place and not have to work on the ranch, or maybe partner up with someone who would help him take it to the next level.

Yet today all he could think about was MacKenzie and he didn't believe those visions would make good welding art for home decor. He smirked to himself, his smile growing as he remembered how MacKenzie had felt in his arms. How that kiss had rocked him to the core just like their first kiss when they were teenagers. There was one recurring thought he wished he could eradicate—she didn't even want to be friends with him. His shoulders rounded and he pushed at his hair, smearing some hay dust onto his forehead and making himself sneeze. He shook his head. He needed to focus on the ranch and his welding work, not the beautiful woman occupying his sister's house, his sister's store, and his every thought.

His dad's truck rolled up in a cloud of dust. "You done loafing with the sick herd?" he hollered through the window.

Isaac used to get so irritated when his dad would say he was loafing, but it was just the way his dad talked and wasn't worth a fight. His mom had believed Isaac could do no wrong. In her eyes he'd been hard-working, talented, basically everything a young man should be. He missed her and her ability to soften his dad up. "Almost. Once I finish up here, I want to work on some welding projects. I've got a bunch of orders backed up."

His dad scowled and gripped the steering wheel tighter. "What do you think this is? A dude ranch? We don't take time off to make pretty flowers. There's fence up the canyon to mend."

Isaac sighed. He made sure this ranch ran like clockwork and he rarely took any time off. If he would've told his dad he was going on a date or even going fishing with buddies, he would've smiled and said to go. For some reason, his dad wasn't supportive of Isaac's art and thought it was a waste of material and time. "Dad. I'm making good money selling my work online."

"Great. Do it after you fix my blasted fence."

"Yes, sir." Isaac stalked to the stack of hay and picked up another bale with each hand. He needed to get his own house and move his equipment and be done with the ranch, but he didn't have enough saved yet and he never would if he kept working fourteen-hour days for his dad. Yet how did he tell the man who had raised him and supported him in everything but welding his entire life that he was quitting? Especially now that Mom was gone and Haley and Taz weren't going to be around as much either. Even though their relationship wasn't great, Isaac was all that his dad had now. He'd work extra hard so he could get everything done then sneak in his shop and weld. His dad couldn't complain when Isaac worked harder than three regular men.

* * *

MacKenzie exited the little house. She'd had a hard time sleeping last night, and for the first time since the murder, it wasn't because of nightmares or fear of closing her eyes and Squire finding her. It was that darn Isaac and his double-darn kiss. Ooh, she was mad at him. If she saw him this morning, she'd tell him off.

Her jaw dropped open and her hand froze on the door handle of her car. Isaac was across the dirt road, hefting a hay bale in each arm as if they weighed no more than pillows. His thin cotton shirt did nothing to hide the muscles rippling across his back and shoulders. The man needed to buy thicker clothing. He might as well have been shirtless. The indecency of the overconfident oaf. MacKenzie hugged herself, remembering the feel of being in those arms last night.

He easily lifted both bales over a fence and dropped then in a trough, sliced the twine with a pocket knife, then tossed hay around to the cows in the pen. MacKenzie's mouth was dry and her palms were sweating.

"Stop it," she muttered to herself. These feelings were nothing, just a physical reaction to a good-looking man. He brushed a dark curl from his face and MacKenzie licked her lips. So what? She was attracted to him. That did *not* mean she liked him. She'd thought movie stars and singers were attractive before and obviously she was never going to date them or be "friends" as Isaac had suggested.

"A physical reaction," she said aloud. "It means nothing." He turned her way as if he'd heard her and lifted a hand in greeting. His lips curved up in an irresistible smile. Her breath whooshed out of her. Okay, it was an intense physical reaction.

MacKenzie yanked on the door handle and slid inside. She revved the motor and squealed the wheels in her hurry to get away. The mistake she made was glancing out the window. Isaac resembled a very handsome, very big, middle-school-aged boy, who'd just been kicked in the stomach by the school bully.

MacKenzie steeled herself against any kind of pity for him. That was the last thing she needed. Match the desire she had for him with sympathy and she'd crawl around begging him to be friends and let him walk all over her with his imperious attitude. It was not happening. She pushed the old Accord to its limits, driving south into town and was going much too fast when she noticed the flashing lights in her rearview. She blinked her eyes against the annoying light as the bottom dropped out of her stomach.

"Oh, crap. Oh, crap. Oh, crap." She could not be getting caught by a policeman. She didn't have a driver's license or any kind of identification. The hair on her neck stood on end. What if the policeman figured out who she was and turned her over to the FBI? What if Tureen had really killed Klein and he came for her? Even if Tureen was gone, she didn't know who to trust. Oh, this was bad, this was so bad.

She pulled over because there was no hope of the Honda outrunning the shiny police car. A nice-looking man, about her age, came up to the open window. He grinned at her, brown eyes twinkling. "Hey. You're Haley's friend."

MacKenzie attempted to smile, afraid it came out as more of a grimace. *Calm down, calm down.* "Yep. I came to run Sugar 'n Spice for her this summer. Wanted to get away from the city and the heat."

"Smart. It's great to see you again." He pointed at himself. "Josh Crusie. We danced once when you visited years ago." His smile broadened. "Then Isaac set his sights on you and it was all over."

So this guy remembered Isaac had liked her all those years ago, but Isaac had never given any indication that he remembered their teenage romance. Just because Isaac had been amazing then he definitely was not now. Her blood pressure spiked as she thought about the kiss from years ago *and* the kiss from last night. How dare he make her fall for his tricks again? Ooh, that man ticked her off.

The policeman rested his elbows on the window frame and leaned in. "You were going pretty fast."

"Yeah. Sorry," her voice squeaked. Now he would take her into custody and the FBI would arrive as soon as he put her fingerprints into the system or whatever they did. Unless Klein had survived and ferreted Tureen and whoever he was working with out, she was as good as turned over to Solomon Squire and dead by nightfall.

Josh cocked an eyebrow. "Don't you have an excuse? Everyone always has an excuse."

MacKenzie shook her head, sweating palms stuck to the steering wheel. "I was ticked at Isaac and not paying attention to anything."

Josh roared at that. "Isaac's a good guy, but I've been ticked at him a time or two myself."

"Are you … good friends?"

"Oh, yeah. Always been friends. I remember how long he mooned over you after you left. Driving us all crazy, wishing you'd come back to town. Begging Haley to give him your number, but she claimed she'd lost it or something. I don't think she liked the idea of her brother going after her friend."

MacKenzie's mouth fell open and she couldn't close it. "Isaac mooned over me? He didn't even act like he remembered that we'd kissed." Her face heated up. What was she saying? And to Isaac's friend, no less.

Josh laughed at that. "Oh, he remembered." Josh straightened up and slapped the car with his hand. "Well, slow down and I'll forget I saw you. Unless you want me to tell Isaac that you remembered him kissing you back in the day."

"No!" MacKenzie shook her head, clinging tighter to the wheel. "Please don't."

He chuckled and held up both hands. "Okay. I won't. Take care now." He gave her a two-finger salute and then strode back to his car.

MacKenzie wilted into her seat. She'd just dodged a huge bullet and she knew she should be grateful Josh hadn't asked for her license or anything, but she could only think of his revelations. Isaac had wanted to call her? Isaac had told his friend about liking her and kissing her as a teenager? Part of her wanted to scream with joy, the other part wanted to find him and slug him. She slowly drove into town, forcing herself to go to work and give herself a chance to decide which part she'd act on.

CHAPTER SIX

MacKenzie said goodbye to the elderly lady and her forty-something daughter. The two had about bought the store out. She gave a happy squeal after the door shut. If she kept selling like this, Haley would have to teach her how to do ordering as well. She missed being at home, teaching her second-grade students and training for Spartan races, but it felt good to be productive again. Thankfully, school wouldn't start for another seven weeks so at least her students wouldn't be thinking she was dead.

She sank into the chair, a satisfied grin on her face.

The door squeaked open and she called out, "Hello, welcome to Sugar 'n Spice."

Brad strutted in, white teeth flashing against his tanned skin. "So are you the sugar or the spice?"

MacKenzie fought to keep her face neutral. She couldn't smile at this guy, after learning what he'd done to her friend. How was she going to kick him out of the store? "I think you should leave." Might as well be direct.

Brad's lips turned down but he recovered with an easy chuckle. "Guess you're the spice."

"Please leave."

Brad ignored her request and strode to the desk. "I thought we had a great time last night. What's going on?"

Guess he was going to be direct also. "Haley called." She arched an eyebrow.

He watched her carefully, no indication of the guilt he should feel. Several seconds passed and the silence became heavy. "And?" he finally prompted.

"And I know all about … what you did to her."

He tilted his head to the side. "That I'm Taz's father?"

35

"Yes." She nodded. "And it wasn't consensual."

Brad's face filled with sadness. "Is she still stuck on that story?" He took a long breath. "That was a really bad night, MacKenzie. We both had too much to drink and we were young and dumb. Look, I shouldn't have let things go as far as they did, but I know she was willing. You have to believe I would never take advantage of a woman." He paused and searched her eyes. "Can you believe me?"

MacKenzie studied him. Either he or Haley was blatantly lying. She wished she could say for sure it was him, but the honest truth was she had only been around Haley at girl's camp a couple weeks each summer and then come and stayed with her and her family that one time. They weren't the closest of friends who told each other every secret. Her gut said to trust Haley, but Brad's sincere look was planting a seed of doubt.

"The Turnbows have always hated my family. Isaac and Trevor wouldn't allow me to be part of Haley's life, they've always kept her and my son away from me."

MacKenzie hated trying to wade through the truth. Something about seeing Brad bloody and prostrate yesterday had made her want to watch out for him. She could imagine Isaac and his dad being fiercely protective of Haley, but was it fair to keep a man's son from him if he and Haley had both been drinking and allowed things to get out of control?

MacKenzie's gut tightened. She hated herself for doubting Haley and couldn't stand the thought of Haley or Isaac skewing the story in their favor. If they were deceiving to her about this then maybe she wasn't in a safe spot. Here she thought she'd run to safety, but really, what had she run to?

"You know Haley is just trying to make me look bad so you'll date Isaac instead of me."

MacKenzie's breath caught. The thought of dating Isaac filled her with all kinds of desires she had no right to be feeling.

"But you've seen how violent Isaac can be. Do you really want to be around a man like that?"

As quick as the good feelings for Isaac had come they disappeared. Brad was right. She'd seen Isaac hit Brad so hard he knocked him down. Before watching the murder she might've just written off the punch as men having a dispute, but now she could hardly stomach violence.

Brad's shoulders drooped when she still didn't talk. "I'll let you think about things, but please, MacKenzie." He reached out and squeezed her arm softly. "Give me a chance to prove I'm not the monster Haley and Isaac try to make me out to be. I felt a real connection with you last night and would really like to get to know you better."

MacKenzie simply looked at him. She didn't know how to respond, especially with her thoughts going a million directions, confused and worried about the situation she may have put herself in, and feeling guilt for doubting her longtime friend.

"I'll come talk to you later," Brad said.

She managed a curt nod before he turned and walked out of the store.

MacKenzie went through the motions of greeting customers, stocking shelves, ringing up purchases, advising on decorative arrangements, but her mind was somewhere else. Maybe it was time to cut her losses and leave. Where could she go? She had five dollars to her name. She could wait until she got paid or contact her parents to wire more money, but that seemed really risky. For sure Squire or the FBI would be monitoring them now.

She drove home to Haley's house in an almost catatonic state. This morning, after the policeman had pulled her over, she'd been excited and nervous, wanting to confront Isaac about remembering her and their kiss years ago. Now she wasn't sure who to trust or where to turn. Was Brad really the monster Haley and Isaac were making him out to be? Or was Isaac unstable and violent? Should she be leery of her friend's brother, especially because of her attraction to him? MacKenzie's brain was spinning and she didn't know how to pinpoint which one was lying to her or why. She was hiding her own truths so she didn't want to judge too harshly, but it was all so sticky and confusing.

She parked her car in front of the cottage. Easing out of the old Honda and standing next to it in the warm summer evening sun, she wished she felt brave enough to go for a run or even better an intense hike. It would be heaven to push her body and clear her mind. She glanced around wistfully at the verdant mountains. Oh, how she wished to hear that Solomon Squire had been caught and her fears were over, but with the new information Brad and Haley had both given her, she found that there were fears waiting everywhere.

She couldn't bear to sit and stew inside her house so she hurried to her bedroom and put on a tank top, workout shorts, and some running socks and shoes. Maybe if she just ran up some trails close to the ranch, she wouldn't be afraid. Isaac's dad, Trevor, seemed like a good old boy who would watch out for a woman. She'd had that instinct the first time she met him years ago, but now she wondered if she could trust her instincts.

Wandering through the ranch, she remembered Haley taking her on a hiking trail through the canyon to the west when she'd visited before. As she passed a large shed, she jumped when a loud popping sound rang out, like the gunshots that had hit the safe house. Scurrying against the building, she searched for a shooter, but saw no one. The sounds came again from inside the shop. Her heart was beating almost as loudly.

Drumming up bravery she didn't feel, she peeked in the open doorway. Isaac had his back to her and sparks were flying from his welding torch as he manipulated a metal loop. The popping sound came from the torch.

MacKenzie relaxed and watched Isaac as her heart rate returned to normal. He was wearing that darn transparent cotton shirt again, guess he probably had been all day. MacKenzie suddenly wished she hadn't been at work and could've spied on him today in that shirt.

As he worked, the muscles in his arms, shoulders, and back flexed time and again. MacKenzie forgot all about hikes and watched him, maybe drooling a little bit, but she wouldn't admit that to herself.

He turned slightly and must've spotted her because he turned off the welder and took off his welding helmet, gloves, and the weird leather drape thing that had been hanging from his helmet. Giving her a slight smile that she found much too sexy, he leaned against the counter. "Hey."

"Hey," MacKenzie whispered, licking her lips, glad he hadn't advanced on her because she probably would've wanted to touch him instead of running away like she should.

"You going running?" He nodded toward her outfit.

"Yes."

"Do you like to run?"

"Yes."

He smirked at her. Good criminy, she was a school teacher. She was capable of more than these one-word answers. "I like to hike a lot too."

He straightened up and took a step toward her. MacKenzie wondered if she should retreat, but there was only camaraderie in his expression. No indication he might kiss her again. Darn.

"I love to mountain bike and hike." Isaac brushed a hand through his dark curls and MacKenzie wondered if they were soft or stiff. She wanted to touch just one.

"Would you want to go ... together?" Isaac asked. "I could show you some fun trails."

MacKenzie gnawed on the inside of her cheek. If Brad was to be believed, Isaac was dangerous. She'd seen him hit Brad, but she remembered him saying as he did so to stay away from MacKenzie. Had he been protecting her? Haley seemed to think that Isaac should've hit Brad more. Did she dare take the risk of going with Isaac? She would absolutely love to escape to a hiking trail and not worry about her situation for an hour or two. But the past two weeks had irrevocably changed her and trust was in short supply.

"No," she muttered and his face fell. "Maybe some other time." She backed away from the doorway, feeling his eyes on her.

Breaking into a run, she headed to the trail. Her legs tired quickly as she tried to maintain a quick pace up the slight incline. Everyone claimed the altitude was tough and she believed them now. Her head pounded and she felt lightheaded.

Enclosed by trees, her gaze darted from side to side. She was safe here. She was on Isaac's property still and from the reports she'd read online last night Squire was believed to have fled the country. What if an animal, or one of Squire's men, or …

Her breath came in quick bursts and it wasn't all from exertion. Her chest started to tighten.

The bushes to her right rustled. MacKenzie darted away from whatever was concealed in the thick greenery, a small scream escaping her lips. The bush exploded and her scream escalated. A huge bird of some sort took flight.

MacKenzie stopped in the middle of the trail, resting her hands on her thighs and just breathing. "Just a bird, just a stupid bird."

She couldn't do this. All she wanted was some simple exercise and Squire had taken even that from her. She couldn't close her eyes at night. She couldn't lead any kind of normal life.

"Aargh!" She screamed out in frustration.

Footsteps pounded up the trail behind her. No, just when she thought she was safe. MacKenzie leapt into action, taking off further into the canyon. Such a dumb move, but all she knew was she had to run. If the person or large animal coming at her meant her harm, where would she escape? Could she dodge off the trail and race back to Isaac? Beg him to protect her and take her hiking with him somewhere she wouldn't be terrified of every bird in the bush?

"MacKenzie!" the man called out from behind her.

She stopped, sweat pouring down her back and her breath coming in gulps that were quickly turning into sobs. "Isaac?" she whimpered.

He rounded a corner and leapt over a rock as he rushed to her side. Wrapping her in his arms, he rested his cheek on her hair, his breathing ragged. "Are you okay?"

MacKenzie nodded against his chest, loving that he'd come for her. The safety of his nearness washed over her. She had to trust him, she just did.

"I am now," she whispered.

He pulled back and searched her body as if checking for injuries. "What happened? I heard you scream."

"A bird." She shook her head in disgust, wishing she could confide in him why she was scared of everything. "I guess I'm not used to running alone in the wild."

Isaac smiled at that. He kept his arm around her, escorting her back toward the ranch. He didn't speak for a few minutes, then he asked hopefully, "Does that mean you'll go hiking with me?"

MacKenzie's breathing had calmed after her scare and she savored the scent of Isaac's musk and metal scent and the pine trees surrounding them. Isaac would make it possible for her to run or hike and feel safe while doing it. Yes, she still had questions about him and some of the things he'd done and said, but she did know that he would never hurt her or allow her to be in danger in any way.

"Yes," the single word escaped her before she could take it back.

They reached the farm yard and Isaac released her and grinned at her. She had to lean against a nearby farm truck for support. He could divert political debates with a grin like that.

"I'll hurry and change." He turned toward his trailer, giving her arm a brief squeeze on his way. MacKenzie stayed where she was, her arm tingling, hoping she'd made the right decision.

* * *

Isaac could hardly believe MacKenzie had agreed to go hiking with him. She'd been ticked at him after he kissed her and when he'd waved and smiled at her this morning she'd scampered away like he was going to hunt her or something. He'd about had the panic attack she looked like she was having when he cautiously followed her up the trail to the old hunting cabin and heard her scream. He hated seeing her scared, but was thankful for the chance to hold her again. Him

41

being there to help her had changed her stance on going hiking together.

He wanted to take her on the Blue Lake Trail but that hike was fourteen miles and he didn't think she'd want to be out on the trail after dark. The Copper Creek Trail was about nine miles round trip and they didn't have to go the entire way to the lake, but he thought she'd love the Judd Waterfall at the first of the hike, and the scenery on the rest of the route. Plus, they could walk side by side most of the way and talk. There was something odd going on with her. She was far too scared of everything and she had apparently driven that piece of crap car all the way from Chicago. He'd noticed she was wearing Haley's clothes, and he'd never seen her with any kind of phone but the basic Samsung Haley used for the store.

He hurried out of his trailer and found her by his shop. "We'll have to drive to the trailhead. It's up past Gothic."

"Oh, okay," she responded quietly, and he worried she was already regretting her decision, but she didn't say anything and walked by his side to his truck.

He got her door and was grateful he'd cleaned the hay and dust out of his old Chevy truck a few days ago. She was quiet as they drove the five miles to the trailhead. He tried a few times to start a conversation but got one word answers. Why was she being so quiet? His lips twisted. Was it because of whatever she was scared of or was she scared of him because of how he'd reacted with Brad yesterday. Dumb, dumb, dumb. He'd have to be on his best behavior, even if Brad showed up.

He bypassed the lower parking lot and bounced up the hill to the higher lot. She jumped out of her side before he could rush around to get her door. He'd have to be quicker next time.

As they started walking, he smiled to himself. He loved this trail, especially in the summer, hiking through the aspen and pine trees on a path covered with pine needles and smelling of the earth.

The first little bit was a dirt road wide enough they could walk side by side. "Did we drive all the way here just to walk on a road?"

42

she asked.

Isaac glanced quickly at her. "It gets better. I promise."

She laughed and gestured around. "I'm teasing, this is beautiful."

His shoulders lowered. She was relaxing and enjoying nature. That was a relief after her earlier reaction to a bird taking flight.

Isaac looked at the forested mountains and soaring peaks. It was beautiful. He was lucky to live in a valley where everything was centered around being out of doors. They made it to the single file trail that lasted a half mile until they reached the falls. The path was strewn with rocks. He gestured for her to go first so she could set the pace. He enjoyed the view as he walked behind her and was very impressed with her speed. He was breathing hard to keep up with her.

As they reached the first scenic spot on the trail, Judd Falls, he took her arm and helped her down to the overlook. It was almost as much fun to touch her as it was to see the delight on her face as she stared at the falls below. "It's cool to look down on a waterfall instead of up."

Isaac nodded. "It is. Do you hike a lot in Chicago?" He couldn't imagine there was much hiking there.

"There are a few great hikes through the trees, but you have to drive a while to get to them. I mostly run along the lake and train for my Spartan races …" Her voice trailed off and she studied the waterfall and river instead of him.

"You're training for Spartan?" Isaac glanced over her physique. It was impressive, there was no doubt about that, but she was long and lean, not overly muscular like he would imagine a woman would have to be to compete in Spartan races.

"Don't sound so surprised."

"You're just really… thin for Spartan."

They started walking slowly back up Copper Creek Trail in the direction of the lake. It widened so they could walk side by side with the trees on either side, the mountains showcased to their left and the river below on their right.

MacKenzie grinned at him. "I'm not thin, I'm wiry." She said wiry with an Irish accent that made him chuckle, then she flexed and he had to admit it was a very nice, wiry arm.

"Wiry, huh? What's with the accent?"

"Haven't you seen *Replacements*? Keanu Reeves? Goofy football show where the NFL goes on strike?"

He was drawing a blank. "No."

"You should watch it, it's funny, but there's this Irish kicker who has no muscle and he claims he's wiry when someone questions his athletic ability because he's so scrawny. It's kind of a joke with me and my friend who trains for Spartan with me."

He liked being privy to her jokes. "We should watch it sometime, together."

"Maybe."

Isaac couldn't help but smile. He might get to spend more time with her. "I'm still hung up on how impressive it is you do Spartan races. I'd love to watch you compete sometime."

She looked away. "Have you watched them on television?"

"Yeah, I've seen a few."

"Our team is hoping to make it to the finals by next spring."

"That's great, but why are you here then?"

"Um, just needed a little escape before school starts."

His stomach dropped. She wasn't going to be here long. "So you're just here for summer."

"I hope so."

It was just like before when she'd come. He'd been a dumb teenager then but had completely fallen for her. She'd left for home shortly after he kissed her and they hadn't talked in over ten years.

"You're in school?" he asked.

They upped their pace as the path flattened out. He knew most people complained about the high altitude when they came here to hike or mountain bike, but she didn't seem to be affected by it.

"No. I teach school."

"Really? What age?" He knew far too little about her.

"Second." She smiled at him. "They're fun little monkeys."

44

"I bet they love you."

She shrugged. "Of course."

Isaac chuckled. "So, Spartan training has got to be tough."

"Yeah, our team is ripped. It helps me want to step it up."

He felt a sudden pang of jealousy. He'd only seen Spartan races a couple of times but the men were all shredded and seemed to be pretty handsy as they helped the women over obstacles. "Where'd you meet your team?"

"The gym. I might be the most wiry, but I can hold my own, especially with the spears and running." She tossed a brilliant grin at him.

Isaac could just bet she held her own. She'd definitely held her own with him the other night. He couldn't really imagine this beautiful woman tossing spears though.

"Speaking of tough, you seem to be a pretty brawny welder," she drawled out.

Isaac chuckled. She thought he was brawny. *Yes.* "I like doing it."

"Were you working on stuff for the ranch?"

"No. I do home décor—wall art, centerpieces that kind of thing."

"Wait a minute." MacKenzie stopped in the middle of the trail and turned to face him. "You're Iceman."

He ducked his head. "I know, the name's cheesy. It's something my buddies used to call me in football."

She was still staring at him with this look of admiration in her eyes that he really liked. "Your work is unbelievable. People just drool over the pieces in Haley's store, but only a few can afford them."

"Thanks. Haley prices my pieces a lot higher than I would." He imitated his sister's voice, "'If you undervalue your work, you won't ever be a success.'" He laughed, but knew his face was probably red. MacKenzie probably thought he was too full of himself and his work. His dad always called him, "Cocksure. Like a rooster who thinks he's worth more than he is." He knew his dad was teasing, but Isaac didn't like it.

"No, I agree. Your pieces are more than worth it. I googled more of your work online and was amazed. Do you sell a lot online?"

"Some, but I need to do a better job with my website and online store. Sadly that takes money or knowledge and time …" He sighed.

"You should be able to hire marketing or web design help if you sell one or two pieces."

He shook his head and studied the pine trees shadowing the trail. "I'm saving for some property to build a house and shop. Work full time on my welding."

"Get out from under dad's thumb?"

"Yep." She seemed to understand how his dad undermined him. Isaac recognized his dad's heart was good and he just didn't know how to interact with an adult son who was still trying to find his place. Isaac had really enjoyed college and all of his business classes, but when his mom had died and his dad asked him to come home, he'd moved back to the ranch without hesitation. He just wished his dad could understand that he needed to be his own man and he loved being artistic. That was probably a lot of it. His dad had said many a time how artists had "frou-frou brains".

Isaac met MacKenzie's gaze. "You probably think I'm a loser, living in a trailer and working at my dad's ranch."

Her dark eyes were warm. "I don't think anyone would dare call you a loser, Isaac Turnbow."

Isaac laughed at that. Did that mean she thought he was tough or she thought he might punch anybody who disagreed with him? He gestured to the mountainside above them. "So what do you think of the hike?" It was almost as pretty as MacKenzie. He watched her study the natural beauty.

"I love it here," she whispered. "Thanks for bringing me."

"Anytime." He really meant that. He wanted to ask if they could be friends again, but didn't dare bring up that kiss and her furious reaction to it. "So hiking again. Tomorrow?"

She paused and studied him for a minute while biting on her lower lip. Isaac wished he could take control of those lips again, but didn't want to anger her like he had last night. If taking her on hikes was the path to becoming friends, he'd control his urges to kiss her for a while.

Finally, she gave him a wide grin. "Sure, but I think this time you should lead the way so I can admire your physique instead of the other way around." She darted up the trail. Isaac took off after her, wondering how she knew he'd been watching her instead of the scenery.

Isaac tried to keep up with her, but he was huffing and puffing. They were a few miles in and crossing their second river when they saw some people coming down the trail.

"What's up there to see?" MacKenzie asked.

The teenage boys both grinned. Their eyes scanning her fit body. "The lake's pretty great."

"How far?"

"About a mile."

Isaac didn't tell her it was much longer than a mile away. They nodded to the boys and kept walking. Thankfully, she'd stopped running. He was more of a mountain biker and skier than a runner. Even though some of this trail was level, a lot was still uphill. They met an older couple who also claimed they had about a mile to the lake. Isaac couldn't hide a smile when the third group they met, a young family carrying a toddler in a backpack told them it was a little over a mile to the lake.

MacKenzie walked on with Isaac, but muttered, "If one more person tells us it's a mile after we've gone another half a mile I'm going to tell them off."

Isaac laughed. "Like you tell me off?"

She tilted her head to the side and licked her lips. "It is fun to tell you off."

"I feel special."

"You should."

They both smiled, then turned back to the trail and studied their feet on the rocks they were ascending. They met a middle-aged man with a large backpack.

"How far is the lake?" MacKenzie asked, winking at Isaac.

"Oh, bout a mile."

"Please tell me you're stinking kidding me right now."

The man looked confused. "Um, no. It's a pretty good incline for this last mile and then you'll be there." He studied them. "You camping there?"

"No." MacKenzie pursed her lips in the cutest way. "Do we look like granolas who sleep under the stars?"

"Granolas?"

"You know, like people who take care of nature and eat granola bars?"

The man laughed. "I do have a few granola bars and like to sleep under the stars."

MacKenzie gave him such a friendly smile, Isaac was jealous. "See? We're not that tough. We like our beds."

The man smiled, wished them good luck, and headed off.

Isaac couldn't hold in the laughter anymore. "You can't offend anyone even when you try to." *You're just too cute.*

"Yeah." She shook her head, looking disgusted with herself. "I really wouldn't want to offend someone. The granola thing just came out. I'm not usually bratty."

"Oh? I'm not sure about that. You've cussed and offended me a few times."

MacKenzie's eyes narrowed then Isaac started laughing and she joined him. "I guess you like to tease me."

"It's becoming a favorite pastime."

She blushed and turned away. "Okay. This mile isn't going to hike itself. Let's get it finished."

Isaac knew they were really close to the lake, but didn't tell her. They hiked up the steep terrain that was the last half mile then they crested the rise and surveyed the small lake below them.

"Well, it's pretty," MacKenzie said, "But I'm not sure it's pretty enough to justify all that hiking."

"You didn't complain … too much. Did you not like the hike?"

She laughed. "I liked it. It felt great to move my legs."

They splashed the cool lake water on each other for a little while then turned back so they could get home before dark. Isaac really enjoyed being around MacKenzie. She didn't complain, she could tease with him and other people, and she was definitely easy on the eyes. Prettier than any scenery he'd seen and he lived in one of the most beautiful valleys in the world.

* * *

MacKenzie slept even worse after spending a few hours with Isaac hiking. He hadn't acted like a jerk, far from it. She really liked the way he acted, reminding her of the chill, fun guy she'd known as a teenager when she'd come to visit before. Yet, she couldn't fall hard and fast for Isaac like she'd done back then. She was an adult, for one, and didn't need a teenage crush, but the bigger reason was the dangerous situation she was in, and all the lying to Haley and Isaac about why she was here. She'd told Haley she just wanted to escape from the city for a while before school started again. Isaac would probably hate her if he knew she was taking advantage of his sister.

She smiled wistfully as she thought about Isaac and how he'd helped her relax and have fun on the hike after she'd been so terrified by being alone and a harmless bird rustling the bushes.

The next day work passed slowly. She met some tourists from Chicago and it was great to chat about her hometown, though she pretended she'd just visited there. Thankfully, she didn't see Brad at all. She was frustrated that he would blatantly lie to her about what happened with Haley. At least she hoped he was lying because it would be a nightmare if Haley and Isaac were the ones who were hiding the truth. She sighed. Like she was hiding the truth about running from a murderer and crime lord.

She rushed home after closing up the store, and changed into running shorts and a tank top. Exiting her front door, she came up short to see the huge, handsome man sitting on the porch swing. What would he think if she sat next to him and reached for his hand?

"Hey," Isaac said. "You ready for another hiking adventure?"

MacKenzie pursed her lips and tilted her head. "Yep. And you promised that I could follow."

Isaac actually blushed. MacKenzie loved it. She knew he'd been checking her out yesterday and she couldn't wait to return the favor. He stood and gestured to his truck. "I guess turnabout's fair play."

"I never understood what that meant."

Isaac chuckled and shrugged. "In this case, I checked you out, now you get to check me out."

MacKenzie laughed and pushed at his side. His very firm side. Of course he didn't budge. The man was built like a tank. "You're assuming I want to check you out."

Isaac escorted her down the stairs and waved a hand over his body. "You wouldn't want to miss out on all of this."

"Oh, I think I'd survive."

Isaac opened the passenger door for her. "Ouch. What if I wouldn't?"

MacKenzie placed a hand over her heart. "Isaac Turnbow. I didn't know you were capable of flirting."

He leaned in and MacKenzie hoped and feared he would kiss her. She had no idea what was developing between them or even if she should let anything develop. Yet, there was something about Isaac that drew her in. It wasn't just his good looks or strong body. She wondered if she'd misread him and his intentions. Now that she was getting to know him better, he was fun to tease and seemed almost humble and uncertain of where he stood with her.

"I'm capable of a lot of things." His eyes dipped to her lips then focused in on hers again. Those green eyes. They killed her.

MacKenzie wanted with everything in her to see exactly what he was capable of, but she forced herself to turn and climb into the truck instead. His expression would've been comical if her heart hadn't been thumping so hard and her disappointment so strong at not kissing him again. The long lashes framing his green eyes dipped as if he was shocked and hurt by her not continuing the flirtation, but she needed to slow this desire down or it would steamroll her. He still hadn't said anything about remembering her from before and she didn't need a relationship right now.

"What are you two ya-hoos doing tonight?" Trevor appeared next to Isaac.

MacKenzie laughed. "Isaac's showing me the local beauty."

"You're the only beauty I see around here." Trevor pumped his eyebrows.

MacKenzie laughed louder as Isaac grimaced. "Dad. Really?"

"What? I can still teach you a thing or two about flirting." He lowered his voice. "You get a girl that pretty in your truck and don't get a kiss you're a lily-livered loser."

Isaac shut the truck door and lowered his voice so she couldn't hear his response. She sat there trying to decide whether to laugh at Trevor or be half-terrified, half-dreaming that Isaac would prove he wasn't a lily-livered loser.

They drove north of town and up Washington Gulch, parking next to a small private reservoir. Walking across the paved dam, they turned onto a dirt road. Isaac held the gate open for her, but MacKenzie paused at a sign warning that black bears were in the area and how to prevent an encounter or what to do if a bear attacked. MacKenzie swallowed, ready to run back to the safety of the truck. "Um, Isaac? I put perfume on before we left."

His cheek crinkled as if he was fighting a smile. "I noticed. You smell great."

Her eyes widened. "What if a *bear* thinks I smell great?" She'd wanted to smell nice for Isaac, never thinking of a bear being drawn to her. The city girl wasn't prepared for bears.

"We'll run up the trail and get sweaty then they won't come near us," Isaac said.

"I'm serious." MacKenzie glanced over the instructions again. "Fight back if the bear attacks? Yikes. Where are you taking me?"

Isaac smiled. "Don't worry. I can protect you from a bear."

"How are you going to do that?" Isaac probably was big enough

51

to take on a bear, but bears had claws and sharp teeth. She shivered at the thought of seeing one.

"They don't like noise and I can scream really loud."

"Oh, I feel all kinds of safe now." She was trying to tease, but her heart was beating hard and fast.

"If that doesn't work, you just run faster than me. The bear will be too busy chewing on my guts to catch you."

MacKenzie's stomach dropped and her palms started sweating. She'd run after Agent Klein had been shot and wondered if she could've helped him if she would've stayed. No way would she leave Isaac if a bear attacked. She'd fight with everything she could find.

They walked side by side up the dirt road and she tried to follow Isaac's lead and not be concerned about bears but enjoy the peaceful scenery. Aspen and pine trees lined the edges and it was a beautiful walk, not too steep, so she didn't have to act like she wasn't winded while trying to catch her breath like yesterday's hike. It was warmer this evening and she wondered how far they were going to hike. She'd loved the hike yesterday, but wearing Haley's shoes had given her a blister on her heel.

Sooner than she expected, they crested the hill and the dirt road turned to a single-wide path. A long, skinny lake framed with cascading pine trees stretched out before them. "Oh, this is gorgeous. What's it called?"

"Thanks." Isaac grinned as if he'd created the picturesque spot. "Meridian Lake, but the locals just call it Long Lake."

"Long Lake fits. Not much of a hike though," she teased him, secretly relieved they weren't going nine miles today.

"I know, but we did a big hike yesterday and I figured it'd be fun to do something different."

"We'll see." She winked at him.

"If you don't love it, we'll hike Snodgrass to make up for it. The trail's just over there." He pointed to the east.

"Glad to know I have options."

"As long as those options are with me," he murmured. He

gestured for her to go ahead. She mulled over his comment as they walked on the path above the lake. They reached a spot where instead of greenery going right down to the water's edge there were some spots with black gravel where people were hanging out or swimming.

"Hey," a redheaded young man with broad shoulders and an even broader stomach called out to MacKenzie, as he floated on a black inner tube. "How's it going?"

"Good. How's the water?" she called back.

"Not as *fine* as you," the man drawled out then laughed too loudly. "Ask me another one."

Isaac stepped up next to MacKenzie. "I've got one. Why don't you shut that mouth?"

"You know what?" He paused. "I think I will." The man cackled. "Isaac Turnbow. What are you doing, you big stud?"

Isaac chuckled. "I'm doing great. How are you, bro?"

"I take it you know him?" MacKenzie asked under her breath.

"Kyle. Went to high school together. Good guy, just really loud."

"I wouldn't have hit on the pretty lady if I knew she was yours," Kyle said.

"Wish I believed that," Isaac retorted.

"Come swim with us." The redhead gestured to his group of friends.

"Think we'll find our own spot."

"Good plan. I'd keep her to myself too." Kyle raised his beer can in a salute and leaned back on his inner tube.

MacKenzie shook her head and kept walking. Isaac led her to an area on the north end of the lake where they could hike down and get close to the water. Isaac removed his shoes, socks, and shirt then gave her a warm smile before running and diving in.

MacKenzie watched as he surfaced, his dark hair thrown back from his face and his skin glistening with the water. He was truly a beautiful man.

"Are you coming?"

MacKenzie couldn't resist. It was going to be weird to swim in her clothes, but it was actually above eighty today, which in Crested Butte meant blazing hot, and the water looked inviting. The handsome man waiting for her in the water looked even more inviting. She untied her shoes and stuffed her socks in them. She walked to the water's edge in her tank top and shorts, wishing she was a boy and could shed her shirt too.

She walked in, and as soon as her toes hit liquid, she jolted. "That's a popsicle!"

Isaac chuckled. "Mountain lake."

"Maybe I'll just stick my sore feet in and watch you swim."

"Come on, that's no fun." Isaac arched an eyebrow at her.

"Cold water isn't my definition of fun."

"It's not that cold. You get used to it quick."

MacKenzie shook her head, not trusting his judgment on the matter. Isaac swam her way with sure strokes, the muscles in his arms sleek and strong. She watched, mesmerized. It was only when he stood in waist deep water, and then started running her way, that she realized she was in trouble.

MacKenzie gave a small gasp and rushed for higher ground. She stubbed her toe on a boulder, crying out in pain. Isaac was by her side in seconds. He swept her off the ground. "Are you okay?"

MacKenzie's breath came in short puffs. She was pinned against Isaac's well-defined chest and couldn't form a coherent thought. His skin was smooth with the rounded muscles pressing against her arm.

"I, um, my toe."

Isaac's eyebrows lifted.

"Stubbed it," she managed.

"The water will make it feel better." His lips curved up in a tempting smile.

"No!" MacKenzie shook her head. "You wouldn't dare."

Isaac ignored her and ran into the water until he was thigh deep. MacKenzie wrapped her arms tightly around his neck and held on. If she was going under, so was he. Isaac grinned and instead of throwing her, he leapt with her in his arms. They plunged under the water and the shock of the cold had MacKenzie sputtering and flailing her arms. She broke from his grip as they surfaced. The water was up to her neck, but only to his chest. It was so cold she could already feel her arms going numb.

MacKenzie wiped water from her eyes and smacked him on the arm. "You cretin! That's freezing cold!"

Isaac backed a step away. "I'm sorry, MacKenzie. I shouldn't have …"

"You're right, you shouldn't have." MacKenzie dragged her arm through the water and flung it at him. Isaac caught a mouthful. "And now you're sorry!" she cried out, laughing and dodging away from him. She swam quickly out into the deeper water. Now that she was all the way in and moving, her body adjusted fairly quickly to the cold water. She loved to swim and savored the weightlessness and the feel of cool liquid against her skin.

Isaac swam up next to her. "No hard feelings?"

"No. It feels great."

He treaded water and smiled. "I like this no-worries MacKenzie."

She returned the smile, though her stomach pitched. What would he think if he knew how great her worries were? Rolling over onto her back, she floated and gazed up at the wide, blue sky and the gray and white streaked clouds touching the pine trees along the mountain's ridge. Isaac floated next to her and took her hand in his. MacKenzie gently kicked. Isaac couldn't be more right; she also loved this no-worries MacKenzie, but knew it couldn't last.

They swam around the lake for almost an hour then finally made themselves climb onto the shore and let the setting sun dry them as they sat on a patch of grass. MacKenzie's stomach grumbled, but she snuck a peek at Isaac's chest and smiled to herself. He was definitely yummier than ice cream.

"What are you grinning at?"

"You."

"Oh, yeah?" He raised a questioning eyebrow. "You were checking me out, weren't you, Mac?"

"Mac?" MacKenzie sputtered.

"You need a nickname. And you need to admit that you like looking at me." His green eyes trailed over her, sparkling with a challenge.

"Mac! Like I'm a truck or a boy or something. You like fighting with me, don't you?"

Isaac chuckled. "I like the fire in you, that's for sure."

"You'll see fire if you try to call me Mac again."

Isaac reached over and lifted the wet hair from her shoulder then brushed his fingers across the bare skin of her shoulder. His touch left tingles in its wake. "I think you'll grow to like it, *Mac*."

"Well, think again." But she was hiding a smile. A nickname? Hmm. It added a layer of intimacy. "Am I so masculine you need to give me a nickname like that?"

"Nothing masculine about you." He trailed his fingers down her arm and squeezed her hand. "But I'm sure you've been called Kenzie by lots of people. I wanted to be different."

She pulled a face. "Different is right."

Isaac laughed again.

The sun dipped behind the mountains and MacKenzie shivered in her wet clothes. They slipped into their shoes and Isaac offered her a hand up.

"You can put your shirt back on," she said.

Isaac tilted his head to the side and studied her. "I would, but then you couldn't check me out as well."

MacKenzie forced a mocking laugh. "In your dreams, big boy." She walked past him to the trail with his laughter following her. Isaac offered her his shirt when she shivered again. The walk back was happily accomplished with his masculine smell surrounding her, no bear sightings, and MacKenzie able to sneak glances at Isaac's chest when he was looking at the scenery.

They reached his truck and arrived at his ranch northwest of town before too long. MacKenzie was sad their time together was at an end. She'd enjoyed being with him far too much and where she had looked forward to working at the home décor store to keep herself occupied, now she dreaded it because she couldn't be with Isaac until after work.

He rushed around to get her door and escorted her up the porch steps. MacKenzie slipped off his shirt and handed it to him. He tugged it on and smiled. "Smells like you."

She bit at her lip, not admitting she'd thought it smelled like him. She knew she looked like a soggy mess, but Isaac's gaze was warm and complimentary as he turned to face her. "Thank you for going with me, Mac. It was fun."

"Everything but your lame nickname."

He smiled and took a step closer. "You like it and you know it."

She shook her head and arched back to meet his eyes. "You're much too sure of yourself, do you know that?"

His eyes widened in surprise. "I wish I was more sure of myself with you."

"What does that mean?"

"If I was sure of myself I'd do this." He wrapped his arms around her lower back and slowly drew her closer, giving her a chance to escape if she wanted to. She didn't want to.

"See, much too confident. Most men would ask permission." MacKenzie's heart thudded against her chest, her skin tingled from his strong body brushing against her.

"Most men would ruin the moment then."

She silently agreed, but didn't want to stroke his ego.

Isaac paused inches from her lips. His warm breath tantalized her and made her want to pull his head down. "Friends?" he whispered.

MacKenzie laughed. "I don't kiss my friends."

Isaac arched an eyebrow and brushed his thumb along her jaw line. "More than friends?"

MacKenzie swallowed hard. "Maybe. Let's see if this kiss can convince me."

"Oh, it'll do more than convince you."

"Much too confident."

"With reason." He pulled her against his body with his strong hands and covered the inches separating their mouths before she had time to give a smart response. MacKenzie melted against him as he explored her mouth and made her ache to be even closer. Isaac held her tenderly, working his enchantment on her mouth. A couple of days ago she'd been exasperated with him, now she wanted to spend every spare minute talking, touching, kissing. He finally pulled back.

"That was almost as good as our first kiss," he said quietly.

She smacked him on the arm. "So now you're admitting that you remembered?"

Isaac looked confused. "Of course I remembered. How could I forget you or that kiss?"

MacKenzie forgot about smacking him again and instead threw her arms around his neck and kissed him. "I felt so bad that you'd forgotten."

"Ah, Mac." His green eyes took on a wicked glint and his firm lips turned up in a grin. "Every time I've kissed you it's been like heaven wrapped up as a beautiful brunette."

MacKenzie blushed. "Thank you. When I came here last week you teased me about trying to snag a billionaire. I was so excited to see you again and it was like you didn't even remember me."

Isaac's huge frame overshadowed her as he gently traced his finger across her cheek and then her lips. "Believe me. I haven't forgotten this."

MacKenzie sighed as she stared into his green eyes. Suddenly, she heard footsteps coming from the road. MacKenzie clung to Isaac, fear wrapping itself around her stronger than even Isaac's arms. Was it Squire? His men? The FBI? How could they have found her?

"Isaac," she whispered. "We need to go."

Isaac shook his head. "What?"

"He's … found me." She could hardly talk through the fear choking her. Could they make it to Isaac's truck? Where would they go? Would Isaac protect her or would he not want to get involved? So far he'd shown every inclination to protect her, but this was huge. Squire would kill Isaac without thinking twice.

"My dad's found you?"

MacKenzie was jolted back to the safety of this farm. "Your *dad*?"

He nodded. "Who did you think it was?"

His dad spotted them and his weathered face split into a huge grin. "Well, what have we here?"

MacKenzie squirmed and backed out of the comfort of Isaac's arms. "Hi, Trevor. Did you have a good day?"

"Nobody cares if I had a good day." He winked at her. "Don't let me interrupt." He sauntered by, whistling and smiling. "Boy finally grew some nerve."

MacKenzie's shoulders deflated. She was safe. Isaac and Trevor were the only ones here.

Isaac studied her. "Who did you think it was?" he repeated.

MacKenzie shook her head and forced herself not to reach out to him again. She wanted his comforting arms, but she had to be strong. "No one. Sorry, I overreacted. Thanks for the fun time tonight."

"Mac." There was a warning note in his voice. "Tell me what's going on. You were shaking a few seconds ago, and the other night you ran from me like the devil was on your heels. And just yesterday you screamed like someone had knifed you when a bird flew out of the bushes."

MacKenzie backed up a step. *Knifed.* She drew in a long breath and worried her lower lip with her teeth. She couldn't tell him. He'd either be mad at her for lying and bringing danger to his family, or turn her over to the police. Maybe he'd think she was certifiable and just laugh at her.

A sudden vision of Solomon Squire leaning over Isaac and Isaac's handsome face covered in blood brought a wave of nausea. He'd be disfigured forever, if he survived. All because of her. She couldn't do this.

"I did not," she insisted. There was nothing to do now, but run— from Isaac and the comfort of his brawny arms. She tossed her hair, hoping for a snooty expression. "Don't make something out of nothing."

His eyebrows arched up. He put a hand on the door to prevent her escape. "Why are you lying to me?"

"How dare you!" MacKenzie poked a finger into his chest. "I don't lie." Her face reddened but she forced herself to hold eye contact.

Isaac studied her and she almost squirmed. Keeping her back ramrod straight, she didn't even blink.

"Well, you're lying about this," he finally muttered. "Come on, Mac. Who's after you? Why are you really here? Something's going on that you don't want anyone to know about."

"You're such an overbearing mound of muscles," MacKenzie yelled, her fear and defensiveness growing. "Stop calling me nicknames, stop assuming we're friends, and stop thinking you know me!" She pushed past his arm and banged into the house, locking the deadbolt behind her.

"You can trust me, Mac," Isaac said through the door.

MacKenzie sank onto the couch and buried her head in her hands. "That's where you're wrong," she whispered, "I can't trust anyone."

CHAPTER SEVEN

Isaac waited outside MacKenzie's door for ten minutes, but she never reappeared. He didn't know where he'd gone wrong. There was obviously something going on that she didn't want anyone to know, but shouldn't she trust *him*?

He hung his head as he walked home. She didn't know him that well and he hadn't made the best impression since she'd been here. Calling her a gold digger because he hated the thought of her with some rich guy and knew all about the girl's camp pact. Then instead of improving the situation he'd scared her by punching Brad. He smiled to himself. The punching had felt good. But not nearly as good as kissing MacKenzie. They'd had so much fun at the lake and the kissing had been extraordinary. Why wouldn't she confide in him?

He spent the next day branding cows with little break. As soon as he was done, he hurried through a shower, dressed in a button down shirt and the fitted jeans Haley had insisted he buy, and rushed in to town. Usually, he'd spend his rare free evenings working on his metal art, but being with MacKenzie was more important. She'd probably be coming back to the ranch sooner or later, but he wanted to take her out to dinner and hopefully get her to trust him and talk to him. Heck, he'd settle for her spending any time with him.

He walked into the store at ten minutes to six. She looked beautiful in a pink and white striped sundress, tidying up the counter. "Hey, Mac." He grinned at her and prayed she wasn't still upset with him for prying. He needed to earn her trust slowly and hopefully be the man she'd turn to for help.

Her mouth fell open and her light brown skin seemed to brighten. "Isaac. You look, really nice."

His smile grew. She seemed to be a lot more calm than last night. "You look beautiful. I was wondering if you had dinner plans."

"Well, I." She shook her head and bit at her lip.

Isaac got distracted staring at her lips. *Did she say she'd go or not? And how long after dinner before he could kiss her again?*

The door whooshed open behind him and Isaac turned to see Brad strutting in. His eyes narrowed.

"You ready to go, pretty lady?" Brad asked, cheesy as ever.

Go? Isaac's hands tightened into fists. He ignored Brad, looking to MacKenzie for an explanation. *Please let her have a good explanation.*

"Brad and I are …" She trailed off and looked past him to Brad.

"Going out for a special dinner," Brad drawled out, looking smug and completely idiotic.

Isaac covered the distance to her side in four long strides. He lowered his voice for her benefit, not his or Brad's comfort level. "You know what he's done. What he's like."

"We'll be in a public place."

He wanted to shake her. She believed him and Haley. Knew what Brad had done, but she didn't care? She'd go to dinner with the worthless piece of dung just because she was upset at Isaac or for some other reason?

"You being alone with him scares me." That was as stark of truth as he could manage. The thought of Brad hurting her like he'd hurt Haley had him clenched up tight, ready to do battle. This was about more than him winning the girl over Brad. This was about a beautiful woman he was beginning to care about, willingly going out with a known rapist.

She cleared her throat and looked down, whispering, "I'm not as scared to be alone with him as I am to be with someone who asks too many questions." She raised her eyes and met his gaze.

Isaac's jaw dropped at the fear in her eyes. She wasn't afraid of Brad. She was afraid of Isaac. "I won't ask anything," he hastened to reassure her, "You don't even have to be with me, just please, please stay away from him."

MacKenzie simply looked at him, not making any promises.

"I think you need to leave, Turnbow," Brad said over his shoulder.

Isaac turned and glared at him then focused on MacKenzie again. "I'll leave when MacKenzie tells me to leave."

Brow furrowed, her eyes darted between the two of them. "Please leave, Isaac," she said, her voice tired and small, her hands clinging to Haley's laptop.

Isaac studied her for several long seconds before leaning in and saying in a low tone. "I'll leave, but I won't be far away. If you're too naïve to protect yourself, I'll protect you." With that, he turned and stomped from the store, letting the door slam behind him.

* * *

MacKenzie watched Isaac go, immediately feeling the loss. *I'll protect you. I'll protect you*, repeated over and over again in her mind.

What had she done? True, she couldn't allow herself to get closer to Isaac, to allow him to know the secrets she was hiding, but did she really need to be with Brad to accomplish that? When he'd come to the store a few hours ago and begged her to go to dinner with him, she'd finally acquiesced to get him to stop talking and go away.

She'd planned on ditching early and avoiding Brad completely, but then Isaac had shown up. He'd looked so good, his broad shoulders filling out an off-white button down shirt that offset his dark skin. His hair was still wet and he hadn't shaved. The desire to touch his stubble alone about took her under. She wanted to fling herself into his arms and then hang on his every word all night long.

"You ready?" Brad came close and offered his arm. It was all MacKenzie could do to not cringe. She didn't want to be with him, but for some odd reason she had an almost protective feeling toward Brad. Maybe it was seeing Isaac punch him and wanting to help him. Her dad used to say there were three sides to every store—your side, my side, and the truth. She didn't think Isaac or Haley were lying about Brad, but she did feel bad for him and didn't want to judge him too harshly because she was falling for Isaac and only wanted to be with him, yet couldn't because of Isaac's protective nature and inquiries into what was going on.

"I'm really not feeling great tonight." She tried to weasel her way out of dinner.

"I understand Isaac can have that effect." He gave her a broad smile. "How about we grab ice cream for dinner, sit outside on this beautiful summer night, and ease your worries that I'm anything like Isaac claims I am?"

MacKenzie was surprised by him again. She appreciated his understanding and loved that he wasn't trying to push her to be alone or do some fancy, drawn-out dinner. "That sounds great."

He grinned and they walked into the bright summer sun. Twenty yards away a man in a white shirt and navy blue dress pants was bent over a man whose legs were twitching. The man on the ground moaned loudly and MacKenzie gasped. All the images from that horrible night came rushing back. Squire bent over that man as the man screamed and writhed in pain.

MacKenzie started toward them when all she wanted to do was run away. Brad grabbed her arm. "Where are you going? Third Bowl is this way."

"That man. I have to help."

Brad glanced over at the two. The nicely dressed gentleman had assisted the other man into a seated position.

"That's nice of you, but Doc Fieldstone is probably the best one to help old Jay. He has seizures and is drunk most of the time so his medication doesn't work properly."

MacKenzie drew a long breath and closed her eyes. The town doctor and a man who had seizures. Not a torture scene. When would she react to normal situations without assuming the worst or wanting to squeal and run away?

She relaxed as they walked down the block and into Third Bowl. MacKenzie actually listened to the ice cream worker, Charlie's, advice tonight and ordered the peanut butter chocolate chip with hot fudge. It melted on her tongue so happily.

They took their ice cream out back by the creek to eat on some picnic tables. She wondered if Brad was truly the monster Haley and Isaac made him out to be. Why was Brad being so kind and non-pushy where Isaac was tense and making her question his motives to make Brad look bad? She noticed Isaac's truck parked down the street half a block. Was he watching them? The thought was infuriating and comforting.

* * *

Isaac pulled into the ranch yard behind MacKenzie's beat-up car. He'd kept his promise and gritted his teeth through the painful half an hour of watching them eating ice cream while he sat in his truck down the street a ways. If either of them noticed him, they didn't give any indication. Then he followed her home. Thank heavens she hadn't been alone with Brad. He swung open his truck door and forgot every intention of not pushing MacKenzie to talk as she scurried from her car to Haley's front porch, obviously trying to avoid him.

Isaac caught up to her. He didn't touch her, but he shadowed her steps. She flung open the screen door and worked the key into the deadbolt with trembling hands. Several seconds passed and her hand was just growing shakier. Isaac took the key from her and turned it, opening the door. MacKenzie hurried through, glancing back at him fearfully.

"Guess you aren't inviting me in?"

"No, I'm not inviting you in!" Sparks flew from her mahogany brown eyes. "Stop following me, stop questioning me, and stop worrying about me!"

"Mac," he tried again, his voice low and on the verge of begging. "I can help with any … problems you have."

She shook her head violently and one tear crested over her thick lashes and rolled down her cheek. That tear about killed him.

"The only problem I have is *you*. Leave. Me. Alone!" She

65

slammed the door in his face.

Isaac didn't move. How had their relationship imploded from friends and amazing kisses to her yelling and slamming the door in his face? What had he done? What could he do? He slowly made his way to his shop. When all else failed, there was always work.

* * *

MacKenzie parted the curtain and watched Isaac go, tears rolling down her face. She wanted to race after him, apologize, go on a hike, and kiss him until the sun set and rose again, but she couldn't. He was far too nosey and caring. He just had it in him, that protective gene, like no woman would ever be in danger if Isaac Turnbow was close by. She wished she could rely on that, but her problems were too huge and spilling them to Isaac would only cause him and his family more trouble.

The tears turned into a torrent then. What was she doing here? Haley had been so kind to give her a house and a job and if Squire found her here, MacKenzie would be putting Haley's beloved father and brother in danger.

Isaac in danger. Blood dripping down his perfect face. No! She bit her lip, unable to deal with the situation she'd created. She needed to leave, but she had to wait until Saturday. There was no way to escape without money. She nodded to herself and wiped the tears away. No matter how much it hurt to think of ditching Isaac, she was going to leave Saturday as soon as she figured out a way to cash her paycheck without any identification.

CHAPTER EIGHT

The next day dragged by. When Brad showed up at closing time and begged her to come with him, MacKenzie knew she should find an excuse, but she was too tired. He might not be the person she wanted to be with, but he'd been nothing but considerate with her and she really needed a distraction right now.

"Where?" she asked.

"It's a surprise, but you're going to love it. Come on, my truck's out front."

MacKenzie shook her head. "I'd rather follow you and go straight home after. I'm really worn out today."

"Okay, no worries." Brad escorted her out of the shop, waiting while she locked the door. He followed her around to the side street and held her car door and then she trailed his truck northeast of town to the ski resorts and lodges. They parked in the main parking lot and Brad escorted her toward the ski lifts.

Children leaped off of a platform onto an enormous trampoline, people milled around the shops and restaurants, and more children played miniature golf or jumped in a harness that bounced them up and down. Most of the people were going up the Red Tail ski lift with mountain bikes loaded on the back of the seat in front of them. Music with a dance beat was in the background. It was a fun atmosphere that gave MacKenzie much-needed energy and excitement for life.

They walked past both lifts and started climbing the mountain.

"What are we doing?" MacKenzie asked. Crested Butte and the lush, green valley spread out below them. There were large homesteads with ponds to the west. This was such an incredible valley.

"Are you afraid of heights?" Brad asked.

"No."

"Good, you'll love this."

They hiked for about ten minutes. MacKenzie watched the mountain bikers descending the trails and wanted to try that, but when Brad gestured toward a tower with a zipline, she squealed in delight and pointed at the first tower.

"Really?"

Brad grinned, took her hand, and walked her to the tower. "I thought you'd like this."

"I've always wanted to do a zipline."

He beamed at her.

Their guides were both teenagers, one was average height with curly brown hair poking out from his beanie, a grungy t-shirt and cargo shorts. The other was a tall kid with spiky blond hair and preppy clothes. "You our private tour?" The blond kid asked.

Brad nodded.

"Great. You all ready?"

"Yes!" MacKenzie shouted.

They both laughed at her exuberance and the dark-haired boy helped them into harnesses and gave them advice and safety details then they climbed onto the tower and the blond flew across to the adjoining tower as the other kid hooked up MacKenzie.

She jumped off the tower and soared through the air. Squeezing her eyes tight and just reveling in the sunshine and the wind and the smell of pine trees, she leaned back, spread her arms wide, and laughed. The ride was over much too quickly as she slowed then jerked to a stop at the next platform.

She waited for Brad then climbed over a rope bridge to the next tower. This time she opened her eyes and took in the gorgeous view of the green valley below. The little town, the river and small lakes, and all the mountains and forested areas looked like a postcard. She loved it here. Part of her wished she didn't have to leave, but it was inevitable that her stay here wouldn't be long.

There were five separate ziplines and three bridges. They rappelled to the bottom of the last tower and she was disappointed the tour wasn't longer. When she finished, the blond helped her take off the harness at the bottom of the tower. She waited for Brad. He arrived with a whoop and a large grin. He seemed to really enjoy life.

Brad stepped out of his harness, walked to her side, and rubbed her arm. "Pretty cool, eh?"

"It was fabulous. Thank you for bringing me up here."

He nodded, looking pleased with himself. They didn't say much as they walked back to their vehicles through the party-like atmosphere by the lodges. Being back on the ground and not flying through the air, she felt like she'd deflated. How sad to come back to reality and the problems she was facing. If only she could escape on that mountain: zip-lining, biking, hiking. She'd be safe and love every minute of it. She'd take Isaac with her. She smiled at her wishful thinking.

They reached her car.

"Thank you. I loved that."

"No problem." He swung open her door. "Can I talk you into dinner tonight too?"

MacKenzie shook her head. "No, but thanks again."

"Maybe tomorrow." His smile was forced, but she didn't have any desire to commit to anything. He didn't seem to be the villain Haley and Isaac thought he was, maybe he'd changed or maybe they were wrong, but he still wasn't her choice for someone to have dinner with. She'd ruined that choice when she'd yelled at Isaac last night.

"Thanks." MacKenzie shut her door and drove away, looking back at the beautiful mountainside and trying to ignore the man watching her go.

* * *

Isaac had a pounding headache after one of the worst days of his life. Branding cows again was bad enough, but the worry over MacKenzie and why she'd turned away from him just ate and ate at him like a worm burrowing through the dirt, chomping and processing but never accomplishing much.

He tried to work in his shop after downing a protein shake for dinner, but he was making a mess instead of art. Taking off his welding gear, he stepped outside the open door. He told himself it was for a breath of fresh air, but he really knew it was so he could watch Haley's house and see if MacKenzie was all right. He didn't know why he cared so much. If she didn't want to heed his and Haley's warnings, she got what she deserved going with Brad. His stomach rolled. No. No one deserved what Brad was capable of.

Her car was there and a light on in the living room. At least she was home safe. Glancing around quickly, he didn't see Brad's four-door truck. Another relief.

He heard a rustle in the bushes around the side of Haley's house. Isaac's spine pricked with the sense of danger. MacKenzie had reacted very strongly to him being on her porch a few nights ago and his dad walking past the next night. Was someone after her? Was she afraid of something tangible? He knew she was hiding something from him.

Isaac slipped into the shadows around the back of the house, stealthily following whoever was stalking MacKenzie.

He saw a tall shadow rise up and peek through the gap in the blinds in the bedroom. Whoever that pervert was, they were going down.

The front door opened and MacKenzie came out onto the porch, holding a pitcher of water. She carefully poured water on the outside flowers, her eyes darting to the shadows. Before Isaac could get close enough to grab the intruder, the guy jumped onto the porch and slurred, "MacKenzie! I came to see you."

Brad. That loser. Isaac rushed around to the porch.

MacKenzie grabbed onto the screen door, yanking it open.

"Hey, pretty woman."

"You're drunk," she screamed at him, trying to escape into the house, but Brad grabbed her arm and pulled her back onto the porch.

"I just wanna have a little fun."

Isaac wasn't going to let this go any farther. He tackled him from behind. Brad roared and flipped over, swinging wildly, his blows weak and ineffectual. Isaac drove his fist into Brad's jaw. Brad crumpled and covered his face, whining, "Don't hit me. Don't!"

Isaac dragged him to his feet. "You're drunk and you're trespassing." He gave him a shove off the porch. "Don't come around MacKenzie again."

Brad's eyes were full of hatred, but he was plowed enough he could barely walk away. "I'll get you soon, Kenzie." He laughed.

Isaac rushed down the porch steps. Brad yelped and scuttled off their property. Isaac let him go. A few seconds later, Brad's truck motor flared and he gunned down the road without any lights. Isaac pulled out his phone and dialed Josh's number.

"What's up?"

"Brad just tried to attack MacKenzie. He's driving toward town, drunk and with no lights on."

"I'll catch him. Does she want to press charges?" Josh sighed loudly. "Don't know if she wants to go through that, it might turn into a case of he said, she said with Brad."

"I know. If you can catch him driving drunk that'll be enough, right?"

"For sure. Nobody can dispute that. Plus, it's a second offense. He'll have to serve time."

Josh hung up before Isaac could thank him. The thought of Brad in jail was very comforting. Retribution, finally.

He turned to MacKenzie. She was pressed against the door frame, quivering.

"I'm sorry," he began. "I tried to warn you."

She gave a little shake of her head and a sob escaped before she flung herself against his chest. Wow. That was a good outcome for him.

Isaac held her close, stroking her long hair and murmuring soft words, "It's okay. I've got you. He won't hurt you."

After a few minutes, she shakily pulled away and gave him a tremulous smile. "Thank you, Isaac. I treated you horribly and you did try to warn me." She shook her head and then rose on her tiptoes and pressed her lips to his.

Isaac was startled for half a second but recovered quickly, matching her kiss for kiss and pouring all his understanding and protection into her, mixed with desire and passion that he'd never felt in his life. He wanted this woman. He wanted to take care of her, be with her, get to know her. He tried to tell her all of that with his kiss. Her response was strong. He slowly backed her against the doorframe. Threading her hands through his hair, she stepped up onto the ledge and changed the kiss with the added height. Isaac could hardly think straight as he savored each sensation.

She pulled away, breathless. "Thank you," she whispered again.

Isaac grinned. "That was the best thank you I've ever had."

She took a step into the house. "I'm going to, um, go inside now." She released a cute little giggle and touched her lips with her fingers.

Isaac wanted to ask if he could follow her inside like the whipped puppy he was, but she was much too appealing to him. After a kiss like that and the adrenaline of fighting Brad, he wasn't too logical in his thinking. He didn't want to prove himself to be as low as Brad, trying to push things too far or too fast with her.

"Can I see you tomorrow?" He didn't reach out and touch her, though every part of him wanted to.

MacKenzie tucked her long, dark hair behind her ear and nodded quickly.

"I'll be close by, in my shop, if you need me," his voice was low and husky, but that couldn't be helped.

MacKenzie smiled. "Thank you."

The thank you had such sincerity in it. He imagined she was thanking him for watching over her, fighting Brad for her, and that kiss.

"Anytime." Isaac tilted his chin up to her then backed away. He tripped on the first porch step and had to grab the railing to steady himself. MacKenzie giggled slightly behind him.

"That's pretty low," he said, "Making fun of the man who can't see straight after kissing you, Mac."

She laughed louder. "I'm just glad to see there's some vulnerability in that huge body."

"Only for you." He winked and walked away with his back straight and what he hoped was a manly walk. He heard her door close after he rounded the corner of the house. Pumping a fist in the air, he was grateful for Brad's drunken revelry for the first time in his life.

CHAPTER NINE

Haley's dad gave MacKenzie her check Saturday morning before she left to open the store. "You been kissing that boy of mine?" he asked.

MacKenzie's eyes widened and she gripped the check tightly. "Maybe."

"Ha! I thought I saw some smooching on the porch." He leaned closer to her. "Well, don't give in too easily. Make that punk work for it."

"You can count on me, sir." She mock saluted him.

He nodded. "I always liked you."

MacKenzie laughed and almost skipped to her old car, singing as she drove into town. Isaac's dad was a tease and she liked laughing with him.

She found a friendly cashier at Clark's Market who knew Haley and was willing to cash the check, not even asking for i.d. MacKenzie was thrilled to have almost a thousand dollars cash. She could escape. Then she thought of Isaac. He'd rescued her last night and then kissed the bejeebees out of her. How could she leave him or leave Haley's store unattended after all her friend had done for her? Did she really have to go tonight? A few more days couldn't hurt. She'd keep watching the news and pray for Squire's capture. It was rumored he was back in the country, but there had been no indication that anyone knew where she was. Maybe if she just kept laying low it would be okay. She couldn't miss that date with Isaac tonight.

He texted her on the phone Haley had given her.

Meet you at your front porch at 6:30?

I'll be there.

Wear a swimsuit.

Were they going back to that beautiful lake to swim again? That'd been fun. She hurried home after work and changed into one of Haley's swimsuits. Thank heavens they were close to the same size and Haley had told her to use anything of hers until MacKenzie's luggage came. She claimed it'd gotten lost on the flight.

She waited on the front porch, nervous and excited. Isaac strode up, wearing a t-shirt and board shorts. The striations in his arms and calves had her checking him out time and time again. My, oh, my, he was fit.

"Hey, Mac," he called out. "You ready?"

"Ready and waiting." She was so grateful he'd let them slip back into the comfortable relationship they'd been developing before she flipped out and yelled at him the other night. If he tried to press her about why she'd been scared, she didn't know what she'd do, but for now she was going to enjoy this easy friendship. Or maybe it was more than friendship. She'd told him she didn't kiss her friends.

Isaac helped her into his truck, which had two large paddle boards sticking out of the back. They drove a little ways east of town and parked next to a walking bridge and a slow-moving river. After unloading the paddle boards onto the riverbank, he pulled out some sub sandwiches, a small veggie platter, and water bottles. They sat on his tailgate to eat.

"Someday soon I'd like to take you out to a real restaurant." He studied her as if gauging her response. "Tomorrow night?" His voice pitched up hopefully.

MacKenzie grinned as she reached for a carrot and plunged it in ranch. "Maybe. Depends how tonight goes."

Isaac winked. "I'll try to be on my best behavior."

They ate the simple dinner, sharing stories about each of their childhoods. It made MacKenzie miss her parents and sisters, but being here with Isaac was definitely helping avert any homesickness. They cleaned up their food and Isaac carried one of the paddle boards into the river. He helped MacKenzie up onto the board, his hands at her waist to steady her. MacKenzie thrilled at his touch and the timbre of his voice, hardly listening to his instructions. He handed her the paddle. "You feel okay?"

"Sure. This should be easy." She tossed her hair and tried to look overconfident. "I'm a Spartan racer, remember?"

He chuckled. "Good point."

"Plus, this river's like half a foot deep and hardly any current."

"Right here it is."

He maneuvered his board into the water. MacKenzie used her paddle to push off, enjoying the slow-moving current and the crystal clear water flowing below her. There was a bike trail off to their side and she could hear the bikers talking as they sped past. The wildflowers next to the river and stands of pine trees were beautiful. Isaac stayed behind her and she paddled to make her board move faster with the current.

"You doing okay?" Isaac asked.

"Great." MacKenzie turned her torso to give him a smile, but threw herself off balance. Before she could recover, she'd toppled off the side of her board into the knee-deep water. She caught herself before falling all the way in, so she didn't get too wet. The water was bracingly cold like the snow had just melted off the mountain and rolled down this path. She barely held in a gasp of shock.

"You all right?" Isaac asked anxiously. "Can you get back on?"

"I'm fine. Thanks." After all her bragging about being a Spartan. She'd been joking, but this was just plain embarrassing. She climbed back onto her board as Isaac maneuvered closer. She must've not been centered because the board flipped out from under her and she flung backwards, knocking into Isaac. He gave a surprised grunt as he fell into the water, MacKenzie sprawled next to him, dunking herself completely.

MacKenzie pushed her wet hair out of the way and laughed. Isaac joined in. He helped her to her feet. They were both wet and their boards were floating away.

"Sorry. I should've taught you better," he said. "Were you paying attention to my instructions about balancing your weight evenly as you get on?"

MacKenzie glanced down and bit her lip. "I was distracted."

"By what?"

She bravely lifted her gaze, took his hands in hers and placed them on her waist like they'd been when he instructed her. "You touching me."

Isaac's eyes widened. He pulled her in closer. "Oh?"

"Maybe you should instruct me again."

"Maybe later," he murmured, lowering his head and kissing her.

It was much, much later when they were able to catch up to their paddleboards and continue the journey down the river.

CHAPTER TEN

MacKenzie sat on the couch late that night, so scared she could hardly stay in the seat. Saying goodnight to Isaac had been sweet torture. His kiss lit up her world and she wished they could continue, dating and kissing, simply enjoying being together and getting to know each other. He was a great guy. She'd read him wrong at first and wished she could take that time back so they could have more time together, but it wasn't to be. Despair ping-ponged through her.

She clutched her money in one hand and a sack of food in the other. She'd written Haley a short note, semi-explaining why she'd had to leave and another note to Isaac thanking him for the wonderful time and hoping she could see him after her life settled down.

Right now she was anything but settled. She'd found a report online, after Isaac had left her with one last kiss, that Squire's private jet had been found outside of Denver, but the authorities were uncertain where his current location was. MacKenzie broke into a cold sweat just thinking about Squire being that close. Did he know where she was? Was he even now heading her way or was it a coincidence? It was close to five hours drive time to Crested Butte from Denver. She couldn't afford to wait and see.

She studied out the window and finally saw the lights turn off in Isaac's trailer. She fidgeted and prayed as she waited another half an hour then slipped out the front door and into her car. Wishing her car was quieter, she hoped that Isaac was sound asleep and wouldn't hear the motor fire.

As she drove slowly out of the ranch yard, she couldn't help glancing back, or the tear that rolled past her lids. If only she'd never witnessed that murder and wasn't running for her life. But she wouldn't have been here in Crested Butte if not for all the crazy circumstances leading up to her trip here. She wouldn't have rediscovered how wonderful Isaac was.

Her car hit a pothole and there was a loud clank under the hood. Black mud sprayed onto her windshield. MacKenzie slowed down and used the washer fluid and wipers to clear the window. Man, it was thick. It hadn't rained in days so the mud must've been sludge. She tried to bring the car back up to fifty-five, no way was she speeding and risking getting caught tonight, but the darn thing wouldn't respond. It seemed to go slower and slower until the engine died completely.

The car drifted to a heartrending stop. MacKenzie gripped the steering wheel and cussed herself for buying such a cheap car. Then it hit her. The black stuff wasn't dirt, it was oil. She'd probably busted the oil pan and seized the engine. How could she be so slow? Her dad had taught her better than that.

She banged her head into the steering wheel. What now? She popped the hood and climbed out of the car. Unlatching the hood, she stared at the dark engine. Even if she'd had a light she didn't know what she could do if she'd really seized the engine like she feared.

Crickets chirped and a cold wind swirled around her, prickling her skin. A branch snapped in the dense trees to her left. MacKenzie jumped and scurried back to the relative safety of the car. Slamming the door, she hit the lock button and stared in all directions. There was nothing to see, no way to know if someone or something was coming after her. She felt so vulnerable and afraid. Bowing her head, she prayed for help. She opened her eyes, her gaze darting around the unknown darkness. Was anyone listening to her prayers? Usually, she had faith, but lately it had dissipated. Was being safe too much to ask?

Lights appeared in her rearview mirror. Someone who could help? Or someone who was intent on hurting her?

As the vehicle approached, she realized it was a cop car. Oh, man, just her luck. Maybe this was her sign to turn herself back into the FBI and hope and pray Tureen had been arrested for shooting Klein and everything would work out.

With no option, she got out of her car. A flashlight shined in her face then Josh's happy voice. "Isaac is going to love me."

MacKenzie shaded her eyes. "Isaac?" Just saying his name filled her with warmth and hope.

"He heard your car leave and found your note. He asked me and some of the other officers to help him search. You in trouble, MacKenzie?"

MacKenzie shook her head. "I guess you could call it that."

"The car dead?"

"Yes."

"We'll take care of that in the morning. Why don't you come with me and we'll go back to Haley's house and sort this all out?"

MacKenzie felt the fear that had been in her since witnessing the murder flare up. What did she really know about Josh? Would Isaac truly send him after her? "Can I call Isaac?"

"Sure." He leaned against his car and waited while she dialed Isaac's number.

"Josh?"

"No, it's me."

"Mac." Isaac's voice was so full of longing, questions, and hope it about killed her.

"Hey, Isaac," she murmured, clamping down on her emotions.

"Why did you run? Let me help you."

MacKenzie didn't want to do this over the phone. "Josh is bringing me back to Haley's. We'll talk about it then."

"Okay."

She hung up and climbed into Josh's car, grateful he'd found her, but wondering how she was going to reveal her situation with a police officer there. Wouldn't he be required to alert the FBI? Tonight must be her time to reveal all. MacKenzie fidgeted in the seat, really wishing she could run.

CHAPTER ELEVEN

Isaac paced Haley's front porch, his stomach churning. What in the world had he done to make MacKenzie run away? He kept trying to remind himself this wasn't about him, but that fear deep down that he wasn't enough kept coming back. Since his mom had died those feelings had grown stronger. He didn't have his mom around telling him how great he was all the time. He'd graduated college yet he'd never had a chance to go and succeed in the real world, prove himself to this town and his dad.

MacKenzie was also tied to those feelings. At seventeen he'd fallen hard for her, but she'd left and never contacted him again. He'd dated a lot of girls, but no one had affected him like her. Why couldn't she trust him to protect her? What was she involved in that was so bad she thought the only solution was to run away in the middle of the night? He didn't care what it was. He was going to be there for her. If she'd let him.

Josh's patrol car pulled into the drive. Isaac rushed down the stairs and flung open MacKenzie's door. She looked so small and vulnerable in the police car. Her brown eyes met his and he fell for her all over again.

He reached his hand out and waited. Her eyes flickered from his face to his hand then she slowly placed her palm in his. That gesture had him. She wanted to trust, she just didn't know how. Well, he'd stay by her side and teach her.

He helped her from the car and cringed at the fear in her eyes and the weariness written on her face. Was it only a few hours ago they'd been paddle boarding down the river, laughing and having a great time?

"Mac," he whispered, enfolding her in his arms. "What happened?"

She leaned her head against his chest, but said nothing. Josh came around the car. "Why don't we go inside and talk?" His voice was much too serious for Isaac's liking. Had she told Josh what was troubling her?

Isaac held her close against his side as they walked into Haley's house. She melted into him and those protective urges fired over and over again. He all but carried her into the house and helped her sit on the couch, still keeping his arm around her and their bodies in firm contact.

Josh cleared his throat. "MacKenzie, I think it's time you trusted us with your secret."

Isaac wanted to be the one she trusted with her secrets, but he had invited Josh into this and was glad to have the law on his side for a change.

Her head tilted up defiantly and she straightened. "How do you know I've got a secret?"

Isaac had to admire her bravery. Even now she wanted to fight through this alone. How could he convince her she didn't need to do that?

"When Isaac called me to find you," Josh said gently, "I did a search on Haley's Facebook page and found you'd lied about your last name. From there it was a quick scan through the law enforcement system."

MacKenzie wilted against Isaac again. Her body quivered and he rubbed her arm in what he hoped was a reassuring gesture. What was Josh implying? MacKenzie wasn't a criminal. Why would she lie about her last name?

"You fled protective custody," Josh continued. His face sober. "The FBI thinks you're dead. The report says Solomon Squire found the safe house, took you, and they're pretty sure he would've killed you to keep you quiet. Yet you're not dead. You ran from Squire or the FBI?"

"FBI," she muttered.

"Why?"

Her golden skin had turned pasty. She quivered against Isaac. "I can't go back," she whispered. "I don't know who to trust."

"Why?" Josh leaned back and waited.

"If I tell you, will you promise not to turn me in?" Her voice was small and weak.

"I can't make a promise like that," Josh said. "It's my responsibility to turn you in. *Protective custody*, MacKenzie. They want to protect you."

"But they didn't." She glanced up at Isaac and their eyes connected. He tried to convey with his look and touch that he wouldn't turn her in. If need be, he'd lay Josh out and run with her from the FBI or whoever wanted to hurt her.

"Tell us what happened and we'll figure out how to help you," Josh said.

Isaac tried to sit there patiently. Josh was a good guy and he'd help them if he could.

MacKenzie nodded, clasping her hands together. Her voice was so low, even Isaac had to strain to understand and he was sitting right next to her. "I was on a late night run on Lake Michigan and I heard men's voices and screaming up ahead. I ducked behind a dumpster and I saw the Squire brothers. They had this man pinned down and they," She swallowed hard and looked at her hands, "C-cut off." Her body was shaking violently against his. "Fingers one at a time, even though he was trying to tell them what he knew. Then they started carving." She let out a sob and stopped talking.

Isaac's body stiffened. Sweet MacKenzie had seen that? He waited a few seconds, simply holding her close and wishing he could take all of this away. Finally, he couldn't stand it anymore and muttered to Josh, "Who are the Squire brothers?"

"Huge crime lords in Chicago," Josh supplied. "Solomon escaped, right?"

"Yes." MacKenzie scrubbed at her cheeks. "He vowed to kill me because I dialed 911 and his brother got shot as they were trying to escape." Her voice trembled, but she kept forcing the words out. "The

FBI put me in protective custody, but one of the agents was bad. Tureen."

Josh's eyebrows shot up. "You think he gave your location to Squire?"

She nodded and exhaled heavily. "He betrayed us and shot Agent Klein. Klein told me if something happened to him to run and not look back."

Isaac's hand was still massaging MacKenzie's arm, but his mind was stirring at the trouble she was in and the trauma she'd experienced. What in the world? She seemed so sweet and innocent. He never would've guessed.

When the silence lengthened, Isaac opened his mouth to reassure her or something, but Josh gave him a quick shake of the head. He glanced over at MacKenzie and saw she was vacantly staring out the window. Finally, she looked up at Isaac. "I'm sorry. I didn't mean to put your family in danger. I just had to escape and I always felt safe here."

"Oh, Mac." Isaac pulled her closer. "I'm not worried about my dad or me being in danger. We're tough old boys. I'm worried about you."

"What about when Haley, Cal, and Taz come back to get ready for the wedding? I need to go. Squire won't hesitate to hurt anyone to get to me." She shuddered. "I check the news online every night for something about him. Tonight, I saw that he'd flown into Denver in a private jet and they have no clue where he is now."

Josh's eyebrows flew up. "I'll check into that and keep you informed of his whereabouts."

MacKenzie shook her head. "It's not enough. I need to run again."

"Not alone, you don't," Isaac said. "If you think you need to run, I'll come with you."

Her eyes were liquid pools as she gazed up at him. "I can't ask that of you," she whispered.

"You don't have to." Isaac placed a kiss on her forehead.

"Isaac."

He'd never heard his name spoken with such feeling. He wanted to get her somewhere safe, then kiss her until neither of them could catch a breath.

Josh interrupted the moment. "I can understand your reluctance to trust the FBI, but we need to follow proper channels here."

"Proper channels almost got her killed." Isaac flung at his friend. His admiration for this woman was huge. She'd witnessed a brutal murder and escaped from a crime lord and the FBI. "I'm asking you as a friend to help us in a way that MacKenzie can feel good about and most of all that will keep her safe."

MacKenzie leaned into him and whispered, "Thank you."

Isaac held her close. This woman was his to love and protect. He hoped she'd agree.

Josh exhaled slowly. "Isaac, you always act before you think. This isn't some good old boys' escape plan."

"Yes, it is." Isaac insisted. His stomach clenched. He could take Josh in a fist fight, but how much trouble would he be in for assaulting an officer of the law?

Josh rolled his eyes and turned to MacKenzie. "I'm going to do some research. Klein was the good agent who got shot?"

A quick head bob.

Classic Josh. He thought if he ignored Isaac things wouldn't come to a head. Well, he was going to have a battle on his hands if he tried to turn MacKenzie in.

"And Tureen was the mole? Do you know first names?"

His voice was so calm Isaac wanted to yell at him that this was not a time to chat. They needed action. His body coiled, ready to move.

"Marcus Klein." She paused and thought for a minute. "I think it was David Tureen, but it might have been Devon."

"Okay. Gives me something to work with. I'll find out what's going on with Squire and see what I can find out about Klein and Tureen. If by some miracle Tureen has been apprehended and Klein is alive, will you let me turn you over to the FBI?"

"No," Isaac said.

MacKenzie gazed at him then refocused on Josh. She slowly nodded. "If I can be in Klein's custody." She shivered. "That is if he's healthy enough." Her eyes brightened with unshed tears. "I'm not sure he could've survived that gunshot. It was in the chest and it was the middle of the night. I don't think he had a vest on."

"Well, let's look into it, but I think you two need to get out of here for now. If I can connect you on Facebook to Haley that quickly, I don't think it's a coincidence that Squire is in Colorado."

Isaac's stomach tumbled. Squire could be headed their way and ready to hurt MacKenzie and his dad. Suddenly, knocking out Josh didn't seem as important as finding a way to protect everyone. "Should I have my dad clear out too?"

"If he will. Knowing him, he'll just prop up with a shotgun and try to take them all out."

Isaac almost laughed at the image, but he didn't want his dad hurt. "We'll go to the hunting cabin. I'll hike up to where I can get service a couple times a day to check in with you."

"Okay." Josh stood. "Grab what you need and get out of here. If Squire landed in Denver earlier tonight he could be here by now."

Isaac tugged MacKenzie to her feet. "Grab some clothes, toiletries, and whatever food you can find. I'll be right back."

Her eyes were so full of fear it killed him to leave her for even a second. "I'll hurry back, Mac." He gave her a quick hug then directed her toward the bedroom. She went with only one backward glance at him. Isaac called his dad and quickly explained the situation. His dad of course tried to argue about leaving. Isaac almost yelled at him. They could hash it out later at the cabin, but right now they needed to move. He hung up without a firm commitment from his dad.

"Can you help me scout the perimeter quick and make sure they're not already here?" he asked Josh.

"I'll do it. You get what you need and get out of here. You taking horses?"

"It's either that or the wheelers and I don't want the noise."

"The cabin's in a good spot. You can hear any motorized vehicle coming. Go through the stream so they can't follow tracks."

Isaac gave him a look.

Josh laughed. "I know. You're not stupid."

Isaac shook his hand. "Thank you."

"If Klein is around I'll turn her into the FBI." Josh was always honest.

Isaac wanted to do what was best for MacKenzie. "I'm not leaving her side no matter what. Hopefully they'll catch this Squire guy and it'll be over soon."

Josh's eyes gave him the message he didn't want. This criminal was squirrely and he had at least one FBI agent on his side. Isaac's resolve to protect MacKenzie heightened. "Don't tell the FBI where we are until Mac and I have a chance to talk to Klein."

"I can do that."

They shook hands again and Isaac rushed to his trailer. They needed to bug out quick.

CHAPTER TWELVE

MacKenzie packed feverishly, cussing herself for not grabbing the food out of her old car and unable to control the tremor in her fingers. She hurried out into the yard to find Josh and Isaac arguing with Trevor.

"I am not leaving," Trevor insisted. "My sick herd and calves would die if I just turn tail and ditch them. I'll lay low here, take care of the basics, and wait for this scumbag to show up." He held up a hand to Josh's protests. "I'll call you if I see anything, but you know I can hold him off and then we'd have him. If I leave then he comes here, finds nothing, then he'll disappear again and he's still free, able to hurt MacKenzie."

Trevor glanced her way and all three men turned to look at her. Isaac's gaze was so full of caring and protection she wanted to cry. She didn't want to pull them into this. "Please come with us, Trevor. I can't stand the thought of something happening to you."

He chuckled. "Nothing's going to happen to me. I'm too old and ornery to die. If they did plug me, I'd get to be with Charlotte again," he muttered under his breath.

"Dad." Isaac looked so torn.

"Enough of this bull. I've got the horses saddled and you two need to get moving."

Isaac shook his head and muttered, "Stubborn old coot."

"I heard that," Trevor said, winking at MacKenzie.

Trevor helped MacKenzie up on the horse, securing her bag on the back. "If I don't hear from you every morning, I'll be up there to check on you," he told Isaac.

"Yes, sir."

"I'm not kidding, smart aleck."

Isaac shook his friend and dad's hands, muttered, "Thanks," and swung up onto the saddle. "You know how to ride a horse?" he asked MacKenzie.

"I've ridden a few times. My uncle has horses."

"Okay. Follow me. It'll take a while to get there."

She waved to Josh and Trevor and they set off into the darkness. Isaac seemed to know the way and she didn't have to do anything but stay in the saddle and stew about her fears. What if Squire killed Trevor or Josh? What if he found her and Isaac? A remote position wasn't much good if the evil crime lord came in with machine guns. What if Squire wasn't caught soon? It would ruin Haley's wedding.

"Isaac?" she called out softly.

"Yeah?" His voice floated back in the dark.

"We need to let Haley and Cal know not to come. Squire could hurt them too. Or little Taz."

"Okay. I'll call them in the morning when I call my dad."

"I feel bad about ruining their wedding."

"They'll be fine," Isaac said.

MacKenzie didn't even want to respond. Because of her, Isaac's entire family was in upheaval.

They rode for about an hour. There was no moon and the stars weren't much help. It was such a dark night that although her eyes adjusted she could still only see shadows and the horse underneath her. She shivered and wished she'd put her sweatshirt on. There were no muggy summer nights in the mountains of Colorado. It was probably fifty degrees and her hands felt like they were turning to ice cubes as she gripped the reins.

She wondered if Isaac had gotten lost, but then he said, "Whoa," to his horse and her horse stopped also. She heard his boots hit the ground then he was at her side, reaching out to her. MacKenzie swung her leg over and gratefully accepted his help to the ground. Her legs were rubbery and buckled underneath her.

"Sorry." Isaac held her close. "You're probably exhausted."

"Don't you ever be sorry for saving my life," MacKenzie spit back at him.

Isaac laughed softly. "I'm not sorry to be here with you." He kept his arm around her waist and directed her through the darkness, across what must've been a small yard and up some porch steps. MacKenzie felt her way through the dimness with him. He opened the door and helped her to a wooden chair. A few seconds later he struck a match and lit a lantern. MacKenzie looked around at the cabin, grateful to be able to take in the world again. It was one open room with the kitchen and living room connected. There were some doors at the back that she assumed were bedrooms or maybe a bathroom, and a winding staircase to a loft.

"There's no power, but we have water that runs from a pressurized spring so the toilet at least flushes and we don't have to haul water. It might get a little chilly tonight, but I don't dare light a fire."

"It's great." It was already chilly, but she wasn't going to complain. She didn't need electricity if she could be with Isaac and be safe.

"I'll be right back." Isaac went outside and came back with their bags. "Are you ready for bed?"

MacKenzie nodded, though she didn't know if she'd sleep. He took her hand. "Your hands are freezing." He covered both of her hands with one of his and MacKenzie let his warmth seep into her. His eyes grazed over her in the dim light of the lantern and she wished he'd hold her close for comfort and more, but he broke her gaze and led her into one of the bedrooms. A double bed was all made up like it was waiting for her.

"Things might be a little dusty. We try to wash the bedding every time we come and hang it out to dry. When mom was alive, she'd haul it all down to the house and wash everything up, but dad and I aren't that ambitious."

"It's great. We can do laundry tomorrow. Give us something to do."

Isaac shifted from foot to foot and dropped her hand. He set her bag down then studied her with an almost frightening intensity.

MacKenzie was certain he wanted to tell her something, but he simply said, "I'll, um, see you in the morning. Let me know if you need anything. The bathroom's right next to you and I'm just in the other bedroom if you need anything."

"Thank you," MacKenzie said. She waited until he shut the door then slipped out of her shoes, fished her sweatshirt out of her bag and pulled it on then lay down on the bed fully clothed. She didn't brush her teeth or wash her face and she didn't even care. Her energy was gone as she finally felt safe. Safe in a cabin somewhere in the mountains. Crazy. But it was Isaac. The guns she'd seen strapped to his saddle didn't hurt either. She wished he could've just held her through the night, but being alone like this she didn't want to push any boundaries.

Saying a prayer on her back because she was too tired to even crawl to her knees, she drifted off to sleep hoping things wouldn't be awkward with her and Isaac now. Why hadn't he said whatever he'd wanted to say and why hadn't he kissed her goodnight? Silly things to worry about when the FBI presumed her dead, Tureen was probably still around, Klein might be gone, and Solomon Squire was coming after her.

* * *

Isaac plowed up the mountain, MacKenzie staying close behind him. His arms and legs were plastered with spider's silk. It wasn't easy hiking with the trail he'd used so many times being overgrown, but it was doable and he loved that MacKenzie could keep up with him so easily. His last girlfriend, Celeste, would've shown up for a hike in heels and expected him to carry her.

Last night had lasted much too long as he hadn't been able to sleep much worrying about MacKenzie's safety and this awkwardness that had settled between them when they'd gotten to the cabin. He wanted to tell her how protective he felt of her and that he thought he was falling in love with her, but it didn't seem to be a great idea with the two of them alone and her so vulnerable. He probably should've reassured her that he wouldn't bring her to an isolated spot to take advantage of her if that was what she was worrying about, but it was probably more that she was just scared to death. Anyone would be with a known crime lord after them and the betrayal of an FBI agent making them lose trust in the system.

The higher they climbed the lighter the air seemed to feel, literally and figuratively. It was a cool morning so his fingertips were stiff, but his back was sweating from the hard climb. They finished the last few switchbacks and reached the summit that overlooked the beautiful valley of Crested Butte. MacKenzie sighed and it sounded like a happy sigh.

"It's so pretty."

Isaac nodded. "I love this perspective."

"Maybe we should just stay here. I feel safe and I can see for miles around so I'll know if anyone is coming after me."

Isaac glanced down at her beautiful face. He wrapped an arm around her shoulder. "It does feel safe up here, doesn't it? But I promise you, Mac, the cabin is very safe and no one is going to get past me, or my dad and Josh." He knew that was a big claim, but he'd fight next to his dad and Josh anytime. If only Cal could come, without Haley and Taz, he'd really feel the odds were in their favor. Cal was a former soldier and had been a security expert for his billionaire buddy before he became a billionaire himself.

"Thanks," she murmured, not sounding a hundred percent convinced.

Isaac pulled his arm back and called his dad first. Of course there was no preamble. "Everything's quiet here," his dad said. "I got the herd fed. I'm patrolling the property and getting the ammo and guns lined up."

"Sounds like fun."

"You bet it is. I hope they come soon."

"Thanks, Dad. Be careful."

His dad snorted and hung up on him. Isaac let out a strangled laugh. "The guy is nuts."

"Is he afraid?" MacKenzie's voice cracked.

"Oh, no. He thinks this is a party."

"Oh, Isaac. He doesn't know. What if they do that to your dad, what they did to ..." Her voice quavered. "That man?"

Isaac's gut tightened at the thought of what that man must've gone through and the possibility of someone hurting his dad. He still missed his mom and didn't know what he'd do if he lost his dad too.

"Is there anyone else who can help him?" she begged.

"Let me call Josh and see what he's learned, then I'll see about some reinforcements." He hated to bother Cal days before his wedding, but this was MacKenzie's life they were talking about. And maybe his father's. Cal would help. He knew it.

"Hey," Josh answered on the first ring. "No sign of Squire. I'm getting a bit of run around from the FBI. They won't tell me status on Tureen, but I did find out through some back channels that Klein survived. He's still in the hospital. I'll try to figure out what hospital and see if I can't contact him directly."

"Okay. I'm thinking of asking Cal to come stay with my dad."

"That's a great idea, but keep Haley and Taz away."

"You know Cal will be with me on that one, and luckily he'll be the one who has to deal with Haley."

Josh laughed. "Check back in tonight and be safe." Josh hung up.

Isaac glanced over at MacKenzie as he pressed Cal's phone number. She gripped her hands tightly together, watching him instead of the scenery. He gave her what he hoped was a reassuring smile.

"Hey, Isaac," Cal called out happily. "Your sister's going to be ticked that you're calling me instead of her."

Isaac laughed, but it sounded uneasy even to him. "Give her a hug from me."

"Happy to give her lots of hugs, but we'll be there soon and you can give her your own."

"Um, Cal, we need to change the plan."

"Back up?"

"MacKenzie's in trouble. She witnessed a murder and was in protective custody. An FBI agent betrayed the operation and shot another agent, and she ran. That's why she came here."

MacKenzie's eyes brightened. Isaac took her hand and squeezed it gently. She turned her head away and swiped her fingers over her cheek.

"Whoa. So you need me?" He sounded as excited as Isaac's dad had to play warrior.

"Yes. Dad's at the house, watching for the guy who's after her, a Solomon Squire, crime lord out of Chicago. He flew into Denver yesterday but is now unaccounted for. We think he might've traced her connection to Haley. Can you keep Haley and Taz away?"

"Yep. I'm going to send them with Maryn and Alyssa, somewhere safe, and I'll get Beck and Tuck to come with me."

"Really?" Isaac's hope spiked. That was an army that few people would mess with. From the stories Cal had shared with him, Tuck not only had resources and knowledge, but had been through Afghanistan with Cal and knew death and fighting. Beck was a tough guy who'd played hockey in the NHL. Scars and fighting were a way of life for him.

"You're not with your dad?" Cal asked.

"No. We went to the hunting cabin."

"Gotcha. Keep MacKenzie safe and we'll be there in a few hours."

"Thanks. I can't tell you what this means."

"Really?" Cal's voice deepened. "You got the hots for Haley's friend?"

Isaac couldn't help but laugh and tug MacKenzie closer. "Definitely." She looked at him like he was crazy. "I'll call you again tonight when I hike up for coverage."

"Sounds good."

Isaac didn't envy Cal the battle he would have keeping Haley away from the situation, but he knew she would do it to protect Taz.

"The wedding?" MacKenzie asked, her lips drooping.

Isaac hugged her. "Oh, sweetheart. No one cares about the wedding."

"Haley sure does!"

"The wedding will happen once we know you're safe. It'll be fine. Cal's bringing Tuck and Beck with him."

She drew back and stared at him with wide eyes. "What about Maryn, Alyssa, Haley, and Taz?"

"They'll get them somewhere safe."

"Isaac, I can't handle so many great men being in danger for my sake."

"Am I a great man?" He was no billionaire or experienced combat man like the other three, but he would do everything in his power to protect her.

She thumped her hand against his chest. "You know you are."

"Maybe you should give me a kiss or something to thank me for putting myself in danger."

MacKenzie smiled, stood on tiptoes and pressed a soft kiss to his lips. Isaac pulled her in and enjoyed every second of their connection. Their lips were still a centimeter apart when she whispered, "How am I going to thank all those other men?"

His gut tightened with jealousy. "Their wives can kiss them to thank them for protecting their friend."

She tilted her head to the side and smiled coyly. "What about your dad and Josh?"

"Don't you even think about kissing either of them," he grunted out with a low growl.

She batted her eyelashes then let out a cute little giggle. Isaac loved the sound and the flirtation. He kissed her soundly again, feeling much better than he had in the past twelve hours. Everything was going to be okay. He knew it.

CHAPTER THIRTEEN

The rest of the day was a contrast of emotions. Worry for Trevor, Josh, and her friends' husbands nagged at MacKenzie, but being with Isaac was wonderful and almost took her mind off the nightmare her life had become.

In some ways she wished Squire would show up so the waiting and apprehension would end. Isaac was so positive that Squire didn't stand a chance against Cal, Tucker, and Beck, but she couldn't stand the thought of one of them being hurt. She thought about Haley, Taz, Maryn, and Alyssa and her heart would drop, then Isaac would distract her with playing some crazy card game or tease her out of her worries.

It was nearing dusk when they finished their simple dinner of pork and beans and canned peaches. They'd hiked up to the summit again a couple of hours ago and everyone had reassured them there was no sign of Squire and everything was going to be okay. Isaac and MacKenzie sat in the porch swing, holding hands as she shared some of the hilarious things her second graders had said to her.

"I bet all the little boys are in love with you," Isaac teased.

"Of course they are." She flipped her hair and then threw her hand on her hip.

Isaac chuckled. "So I have lots of competition."

"You have no idea." She lowered her eyelashes, feeling suddenly shy. They'd been so comfortable around each other all day and him touching her, while still sending thrills through her nervous system, was becoming a little bit familiar, but he hadn't kissed her since this morning's hike.

"I'd better make sure to be more impressive than the competition."

MacKenzie glanced up at him. He trailed his hands through her hair and to her shoulders. His green eyes sparkled at her as he slowly lowered his head and pressed his mouth to hers. He took his time and she reveled in the movement of his mouth and hands. The crickets chirping in the background, the stream trickling by, and the porch swing all disappeared. There was only her and Isaac. MacKenzie wrapped her hands around his biceps and held on.

He pulled back and grinned at her. "Was that as good as some Chicago city boy?"

MacKenzie tried to slow her breathing. "I thought you were competing with my second graders, but you want to take on the whole city of Chicago?"

Isaac nodded, tracing his thumb along her jaw. MacKenzie paused as if to consider, but when his face got too serious, she had to admit. "I think you could best anyone in the world with a kiss like that."

He grinned and bent to kiss her again, but suddenly stopped. His head whipped around and he grabbed her by the waist and threw her toward the cabin door.

"What—" MacKenzie cried out.

Isaac ripped the door open and shoved her inside just as gunshots shattered the peaceful night. She screamed and rolled behind the door, covering her head with her hands. The door slammed behind Isaac, more gunshots dinging into the wooden exterior. She searched him for blood, but couldn't see anything.

"Are you okay?" she gasped out.

He nodded tersely just as the picture window overlooking the front porch shattered. Isaac grabbed her hand and tugged her to her feet. "We've got to move!"

They ran through the cabin and into Isaac's bedroom. The window was already open. He flipped the screen out, caught her around the waist, and lifted her out. Her feet touched the ground and a second later he'd jumped out to join her. There were still gunshots barraging the front of the cabin. Hopefully they hadn't come around back yet or entered to see their prey was gone.

Isaac took her hand and they sprinted into the forest toward the trail they'd taken twice to make phone calls. MacKenzie wanted to ask him what his plan was, but couldn't catch a breath with the pace they were keeping. Luckily, there was no moon like last night so it was dark enough maybe Squire and his men wouldn't be able to track them. A cold fear grabbed her gut. She'd heard the FBI agents saying these guys had top of the line equipment. They probably had infrared scopes. If they did, she and Isaac had an even bigger disadvantage. Oh, they were so dead!

She suddenly realized she hadn't heard any shooting behind them for a few minutes. Had they put that much distance behind them or had the men stopped shooting since they'd realized they weren't in the cabin anymore?

Her legs burned as they raced for the summit. Bushes and tree limbs batted at her and she kept rubbing at her face that felt like it was covered with spider webs. She didn't know if they were on the trail or just plowing straight up the mountain. The incline needed to stop. It was vicious. Even though she worked out hard every day, they'd climbed this twice today with very little sleep last night and the fear was sapping energy. Whatever happened to the adrenaline that was supposed to kick in and help you go faster?

They reached the summit and Isaac whipped out his phone. "You okay?" he whispered while the call connected.

"Um, no?"

"They hit you?" Isaac's voice pitched up in fear.

"No, just scared," she panted out.

He squeezed her hand then muttered, "Come on, Cal, pick up."

MacKenzie could hear something moving through the brush below them. "Isaac!" She grabbed onto his arm and pulled him down. Luckily he went with the motion or she wouldn't have been able to budge him. Bullets whizzed through the air and pinged into the trees.

"Follow me," Isaac whispered.

He crawled through the underbrush and she trailed his movements, rocks and twigs scratching at her face and arms.

The bullet barrage stopped and a smooth voice called out from much too close by, "MacKenzie? Why do you keep running, love?"

MacKenzie's entire body shuddered. She'd heard that same voice that fateful night. He'd said things in his honey tongue as nicely as could be, while he and his brother tortured that man.

"Who's your friend?"

Feet treaded through the underbrush toward them. MacKenzie kept crawling, but couldn't imagine any scenario where they escaped. Solomon Squire was going to find them, have his fun with them, and then, if they were lucky, put a bullet in their brains. Oh, why had she gotten Isaac into this? Were all the other men who'd come to protect her already dead? Tears leaked out of her eyes. This was all her fault. She never should've come to Crested Butte.

"I've got a deal for you, MacKenzie. You stand up and come to me, and your friend can go. I don't have any issue with him."

MacKenzie's heart leapt. Would Squire really let Isaac go? She could protect Isaac by giving herself up? She'd do that all day, any day. She started to stand. Isaac's body smothered hers and flattened her to the ground. His hand covered her mouth so she couldn't talk. He whispered harshly in her ear, "No! Don't even think about it."

"In fact, I can promise you I won't torture you. I really like the look of you, love. You can choose to stay with me or I'll kill you quickly. I don't torture women, but I would like to give you the chance to get to know me and see if you like what I have to offer." He paused and the silence was broken by crickets chirping and Isaac and MacKenzie's breath, which seemed much too loud.

"Isaac," MacKenzie talked into his hand, hoping he could hear her. He pulled back his hand a little bit. "Please go. It's our only chance. Come back with help."

Isaac shook his head and she felt it against her shoulder. "I won't leave you."

"There's no other way to escape," she whispered. "I'll make a lot of noise so you can get away. You know where you're going. It's our only hope." There really was no hope. Cal and all the others were probably dead. The only solace was Squire might have been in a hurry and not tortured their friends before killing them. Now she could only help Isaac. She'd do anything to protect him.

"No," Isaac murmured, clinging to her.

"Please," she begged, tears slipping past her eyelashes and running hot down her cheeks. "Go get help. Please."

"I'll get help. Stay hidden." Isaac pressed a kiss to her forehead. "I love you." He slid off of her and started crawling through the undergrowth.

Had he really just said he loved her? Not that it mattered now. She would be dead soon. She was alone and at Solomon Squire's mercy. MacKenzie knew a moment of fear like she'd never experienced in her life. What could she do? Pretend Squire didn't make her stomach curdle so he let her live? Or go down fighting? She didn't really think Isaac could get help before Squire either killed her or took her far away where she'd never see Isaac again.

CHAPTER FOURTEEN

Isaac army crawled through the thick brush, his breath coming in fast pants. He'd left MacKenzie, alone. She was right that they had no options, but everything in him ached to rush back to her, cover her body with his, and hope Squire would kill them quickly.

He couldn't give in to this despair. He couldn't quit on MacKenzie. A light flicked on. MacKenzie tripped and went down. For one second, Isaac could see MacKenzie's beautiful face through the bushes. His stomach turned to ice at the terror in her eyes. He wanted to run to her, but forced himself to be smart and keep moving for a better position.

Protect MacKenzie was the only thought that tumbled through his mind. He prayed like he'd never prayed in his life then circled around behind Squire's men. His chances weren't great. Six armed men against a ranch hand, but he'd fight until they killed him.

* * *

MacKenzie said a quick prayer then jumped to her feet and started stomping toward the direction she'd heard Squire's voice. *Protect Isaac. Protect Isaac*, she repeated over and over again. The cause kept the fear at bay. Her fingers burned like they sensed they might be severed soon. She flinched with each step, fully expecting bullets to riddle her body. At least it would be better than a knife. Nausea rushed up her throat. She retched in the grass, wiped her mouth with the back of her hand, and forced herself to place one foot in front of the other.

"Where are you?" she called out. Her voice gyrated. Cold sweat puddled in her bra. *What was she doing?* Had Isaac really left her or would he come back? She wanted Isaac to be safe. She would take the torture and pain to give Isaac a chance to live.

A light hit her face, blinding her. She tripped over some undergrowth and went down. She gave into the fear at that moment and almost broke down sobbing. Forcing herself to stand, she walked toward the light. As she got closer, the light was lowered and she could see that it was attached to a large gun, held by a man in black clothing. She counted five men plus Squire, standing in the middle of the semicircle, grinning. They all had goggles on their heads. Infrared or thermal imaging? All she knew was they could see in the dark like she'd feared.

"You listened," Squire said. "That's a good girl. I think we're going to get along just fine."

MacKenzie's heart was thrumming so hard she felt like it was in her throat. Her mouth burned from the acid of her vomit. Her vision blurred from tears she didn't want to deal with right now. Her legs were weak like she'd run twenty miles through the mud.

Squire gestured her forward. "Come now. It's time to get out of here before the boyfriend actually finds some help." He gestured with his head to two of his men. They nodded and started in the direction Isaac had disappeared.

"You said you'd let him go," MacKenzie squeaked past her dry throat.

Squire grabbed her arm and pulled her close. His white teeth flashed against perfectly tanned skin and his spicy cologne made her want to gag. He was a good-looking, put-together, completely disgusting man. "Oh, love. What fairy tale are you living in?"

Isaac. She wanted to scream and cry for him. What would those men do when they caught him? He would fight and they'd hurt him and kill him. Isaac was tough, but no match for trained mercenaries. She glanced at the three remaining men and gasped when she recognized Tureen.

He tilted up his chin. "Good to see you."

"I wish I could say the same."

Squire laughed. He traced a hand down her face and she flinched away from his fingers. He tsked. "I told you the deal. You give me a chance and I'll let you live, or you can choose to die quickly right now."

MacKenzie tilted her chin up and glared at him, though her trembling body contradicted the confidence she tried to display. "What fairy tale are you living in?"

He looked surprised for half a second then he chuckled. "A little spice and bravado is always worth keeping around." He nodded to his men. "Let's go. Kill that light."

The light went out. Keeping his arm around MacKenzie's waist, Squire flicked a switch on his goggles and led the way along the mountainside. Away from the cabin, she thought, but she was getting confused in the dark. MacKenzie's arms and legs were thrashed by branches even through her jeans and she tripped repeatedly on rocks and roots. Squire kept jerking her to her feet. She would've rather face-planted than have him touching her.

She had no clue where they were going. Why wouldn't they go back down the hill to the cabin? These men had to have vehicles there. Then she heard the steady thrum of a chopper and her stomach tumbled. The small hope she'd clung to shattered. Isaac was never going to get to her in time.

There was a loud thud behind her. MacKenzie whipped around but couldn't see anything.

"Beau?" she heard one of the other men whisper harshly. "Where are—" His question was cut off and then it sounded like he rolled down the mountain.

Squire whipped around and pinned Mackenzie in front of him. "Beau? Liam? Tureen?"

MacKenzie blinked in surprise. She couldn't see anything, but it was obvious Squire's men were not with them anymore. Did she dare hope? Isaac? She didn't waste time thinking about it, but jabbed her elbow hard into Squire's gut. He jerked in surprise and loosened his grip. She jumped down on his instep and he howled in pain, then she thrust her fist into the underside of his jaw before dropping to the ground and rolling away from him. Lights suddenly appeared on several guns and Squire cried out and tore off his goggles.

He was surrounded by Cal, Isaac, Beck, Tucker, Josh, and Trevor. MacKenzie scurried on the ground toward Isaac. He picked her up and hugged her fiercely. "Good fighting, babe."

"You learn a thing or two when you're a Spartan." Her trembling voice gave away how shaken up she was. Isaac held her close and kissed her forehead.

Squire was looking nervously at the group of them. "How'd you find us?"

"We have a bit of combat experience." Cal arched an eyebrow. "You idiots left your Land Rover in a ditch with hardly any covering."

Solomon's eyes darted to his chopper.

"Thanks again." Cal lifted a vicious-looking weapon and riddled the chopper with bullets. The pilot took off and within seconds the thrumming of his rotors faded in the distance. Cal smiled. "So, Squire. How do you want to play this?"

Squire held on to his gun, his eyes darting nervously around the group. MacKenzie clung to Isaac, but she also looked around. These were big, well-armed men, and it was obvious they were ticked off.

"I don't like to lose," Squire said. He lifted his gun. Cal fired before Squire could even pull the trigger. Squire screamed in agony, blood spraying from his forearm. He dropped the gun and continued screaming.

Cal marched over, kicked the gun aside, and grabbed Squire's uninjured arm. "Stop whining," he muttered. "I've heard about some of the stunts you've pulled and you're lucky I don't start cutting off your fingers."

He dragged Squire down the mountainside. Josh and Tucker following close behind. Beck glanced over at MacKenzie. "You okay?"

She nodded. "Yes. Thank you." Her voice caught. She couldn't express how grateful she was to all of these men. "Wait! There are two more men. They followed Isaac."

Beck chuckled. "They're out of commission for a little while.

Josh put a call in and the county's sending their entire sheriff's department to round all of them up. We'll grab the ones we see as we go down."

Beck followed the others. Isaac's dad squeezed her arm. "You are one tough chick. Remind him never to tick you off." He pointed at Isaac and laughed.

She smiled in response. Trevor also took off down the mountainside. MacKenzie started to follow, but Isaac held her against his chest.

"Thank you," she said. "You came back. You rescued me." She shuddered as the fear left her body and gave him a hard kiss on the mouth. "Thank you."

Isaac smiled gently at her. "You did a pretty good job of rescuing yourself." He kissed her again and she melted against him, wishing she could stay in this spot forever.

Isaac was yanked from her and he skidded down the mountain. She gasped as she stared into the furious eyes of Agent Tureen. Tureen grabbed at her. MacKenzie kicked him in the thigh. His leg buckled. He cursed, but kept coming.

Isaac thundered up the hill and plowed into Tureen. They slammed to the ground and MacKenzie could hardly see the scuffle in the dark. She prayed Isaac had the upper hand and wished she knew what she could do to help.

A gunshot rang out and she screamed. Had Tureen shot Isaac? She scrambled on hands and knees toward the men who seemed to have stopped fighting. "Isaac?" she begged. "Be okay, please be okay."

"I'm good," he said. "I choked him out."

MacKenzie stood and Isaac was at her side. "What was the shot?"

"It was below us. Let's go." He grabbed Tureen's arm and dragged him behind them.

MacKenzie would've felt bad for anyone else but Tureen. The corrupt agent wakened and moaned in agony. They both ignored him. They saw lights ahead and reached the group of men, plus some of the

Sheriff's Department. One of the deputies came over and took Tureen from Isaac's grasp. "Thanks," Isaac muttered.

"We've almost got them all."

"Good luck." He gestured with his chin. "What happened?"

"Squire tried to escape."

Cal looked up at them with haunted eyes. Solomon Squire was on the ground next to him, not moving. "I didn't kill him. You saw how I shot his arm earlier instead of taking the kill shot?"

Isaac nodded. "We all saw that, Cal."

Tucker clapped his large hand on his friend's shoulder. "You didn't kill him." He glanced at Isaac and MacKenzie. "Squire grabbed Cal's gun and Cal was able to fight him off then Squire pulled the trigger." He shook his head. "Killed himself."

MacKenzie shuddered, envisioning the death. She'd had enough death to last her an eternity.

The group was somber as they climbed on off-road vehicles and horses and made their way down the mountainside. Thankfully, the Sheriff's department took care of Squire's men. They all convened at Trevor's house and answered questions. Then the FBI showed up and the questions started all over again.

"Well, look who's alive and kicking," the familiar voice drawled from the entryway.

MacKenzie jumped to her feet and rushed to hug him. Klein grunted. "Softly now."

"You're alive!"

"Barely."

"But how?"

"Tureen took off after you and I guess one of the other agents found me. It's been pretty touch and go, but I got out of intensive care last week and Tureen was gone before I could turn him in. Glad you're okay."

Isaac was by her side. He reached out his hand. "Isaac Turnbow, sir. MacKenzie said you were the only one she could trust."

Klein's white teeth flashed against his dark skin. "I don't know about the only one, but I am pretty trustworthy. Nice to meet you."

"Something's bugging me," Isaac said. "How did Squire find MacKenzie and I at the cabin and avoid Cal and the others?"

Klein looked him over. "Do you know a Brad Hall?"

Isaac's fists clenched. "Too well."

"Supposedly he made bail yesterday and was spouting all over town about how he was going to get back at you and MacKenzie. One of Tureen's men got the layout of your ranch and the information about your hunting cabin from him at a bar last night." Klein grinned at the furious expression on Isaac's face. "I know that look. Don't worry. He'll be locked up for a long time. Hopefully long enough you won't still want to thrash him when he gets out."

"I doubt that," Isaac muttered.

Klein laughed and inclined his head to MacKenzie. "Walk me outside?"

She walked out into the chilly night with him. So tired that she was barely functioning, she wondered if it was almost morning. Klein stopped next to a black sport utility vehicle. "You did good running. Tureen didn't leave until a week after you disappeared and he found out I'd been able to talk and tell the director he was the mole. He would've given you to Squire if you would've stuck around."

A cold shiver raced through her. Squire was dead. It was awful to feel relief at another person's demise, but she still felt it.

"With Squire gone, you're welcome to go back to your life."

MacKenzie nodded. Back to Chicago. A movement on the porch caught her eye. Isaac stood there, his large frame outlined by the porch light. She could've sworn he'd told her he loved her before he'd crawled away back on the mountain, but was it just a reaction? A thing someone says when they're certain you're going to die?

Klein followed her gaze and chuckled. "I see. Well, if you want to fly home, someone will come for you in the morning. Maybe you should at least go visit your parents and tell them you're thinking about relocating."

MacKenzie ignored the insinuation and gave him a quick hug.

"Thank you."

"It's been a pleasure." He nodded and climbed into the car.

MacKenzie walked toward the porch as Isaac descended the stairs. He took her elbow and led her to Haley's house. "You look tired."

"Such a compliment," she tried to joke, but inside she was churned up. She was safe now. Such a relief in every way, but safety demanded decisions she didn't want to make.

"You look beautiful." He smiled. "And very tired." He walked her into Haley's house and proceeded to check each room.

"What are you doing? Didn't the Sheriff's office get them all?"

"They did. I just want you to feel safe." His green eyes focused in on her and MacKenzie felt safe, and a whole lot of other emotions.

"Thank you, Isaac." It was all she could manage as her throat closed off.

He gave her an all-too-brief hug and peck on the lips then ushered her to the bed. "Get some rest. We can talk tomorrow."

MacKenzie sank into the soft mattress and feeling every bit of her exhaustion, though she didn't want Isaac to leave.

He removed her shoes, giving her that confident grin of his. The smolder in his eyes warmed her to her core. Placing one hand on each side of her shoulders, he lowered his upper body until his mouth was inches from hers. "Are you doing okay?"

MacKenzie licked her lips and focused on his handsome face. How like Isaac to worry about her. "How could I not be with you around?"

He grinned and gently brushed his lips with hers. MacKenzie wrapped a hand around the back of his neck and arched up to meet him. The kiss turned from comfort to passion in milliseconds. Isaac groaned and lowered his upper body onto hers. MacKenzie gasped from the wonderful pressure. The joy of Isaac surrounding her.

He broke the kiss and quickly stood. Staring at her, his eyes filled with a desire she knew was mirrored in her own. He cleared his throat and backed away a step. Disappointment shot through MacKenzie, but gratitude for Isaac's self-control slowly overruled the ache to stay in his arms.

"Thank you," she whispered.

He nodded. "The next kiss needs to be in a safer spot."

MacKenzie gave a chortled laugh. "Good plan."

Isaac brushed a hand down her cheek then turned and walked out the door. MacKenzie sighed. *Oh, Isaac.* He was strong in every way that mattered to her. She was in love with that man and she had to go home in the morning. What was she going to do?

CHAPTER FIFTEEN

MacKenzie woke to a banging on the door. A glance at the clock showed 6:23 a.m. Her limbs were heavy and her head felt like it'd been smacked with a club repeatedly. Three hours of sleep was not enough. She slipped out of bed and forced one foot in front of the other to the front door. Then the realization of who it must be brought her more awake and a smile to her face.

"Isaac," she said, swinging the door wide. Her smile dropped. "Agent Klein?"

He chuckled. "Happy to see me?"

MacKenzie glanced around in confusion. There was an agency car waiting, but she didn't see Isaac, Trevor, or any of her friends' husbands. "What's going on?"

"I told you we could get you back to Chicago, but the plane leaves from Gunnison in an hour."

"It's 6:23 in the morning."

"Yep."

"No wonder I feel like somebody beat me with a baseball bat."

He smiled. "I should've called, but I didn't have a number for you. You want to go home?"

MacKenzie debated for half a second. Home. The very word sounded wonderful. Her parents. Her sisters. Her training partners. Her friends. Her students. But this little town in Colorado and a large, dark-haired man had her heart. She wanted to stay, but then her parent's faces flashed into her mind. They needed to hug her, talk to her, see for themselves she was okay. She should go home and figure some things out.

"Yeah." She nodded. "Give me a minute." She raced into the bedroom, but there was nothing of hers. She'd been borrowing Haley's clothes and everything else. After making the bed and quickly

110

wiping down the bathroom, she washed her face, brushed her teeth, and hurried back to the living area. Klein still waited outside the open front door.

She wanted to wake Isaac up and explain why she had to go and that she'd be back soon, but he'd done so much for her and the poor man needed to sleep. She settled for a note.

Isaac,

Thank you for everything. You saved my life and gave me some wonderful memories. I'm going to Chicago to see my parents and figure out some things with school and my training partners. I'll be back for Haley's wedding. Can't wait to be with you again.

Thanks,

MacKenzie

She debated over scratching out the thanks and putting, love, but that seemed a little forward. They'd shared a lot and she wasn't sure where they stood. She hated to leave without saying goodbye, but she'd be back in a few days.

Running past Klein, she put the note on Isaac's windshield. Hopefully he wouldn't think she'd ditched him and hate her.

* * *

Isaac woke late. His body hurt from all the hiking, fighting, and not sleeping well. MacKenzie. The thought of the raven-haired beauty set his pulse skittering. He jumped out of bed, took a quick shower, not bothering to shave, brushed his teeth, and was out the door. They were going to talk today. Did he dare tell her he loved her again? The words spoken last night as he scurried away to try and save her didn't seem to be validated as she hadn't responded like she'd even heard him. Yet he still felt those words inside. It was real and he wanted to tell her. He wanted to go to Chicago with her and meet her family, then pack up her stuff and bring her back here. Home. With him.

He knocked on Haley's front door, but there was no response. Waiting for what he hoped was an appropriate lapse, he knocked twice more before twisting the doorknob and pushing it open. "Mac?" he called out, his voice echoing strangely in the small house.

He walked through the rooms, but he already knew she wasn't there. Maybe she'd gone for a run or … what? Striding out of the house, he paced the yard then went to his truck, ready to go search for her. A white piece of paper fluttered underneath his wipers. As if in a trance, he pulled it out, read it, then crumpled it up. Back to Chicago? Without saying goodbye? It was a punch in the gut.

He paced around the yard, the note clutched in his hand. His dad walked out of the barn and eyed him strangely. "What's in your craw?"

Swallowing hard, Isaac formed the words. "MacKenzie," he cleared his throat, "went back to Chicago."

His dad stared at him for several seconds then shrugged. "So go after her. You don't win the girl by being a wuss." Then he walked back into the barn.

Isaac sat there, a plan forming in his head. She said she was coming back for the wedding, but he wanted to be with her now. Was it too bold? Him going to Chicago? Maybe, but in his dad's words, *You don't win the girl by being a wuss*.

No one would call Isaac a wuss. He hurried toward to his trailer to pack a bag. This was going to cut into his savings for his business, but if it showed MacKenzie how much she meant to him, it would be worth it.

"Isaac," Cal's voice rang through the yard.

Isaac turned and waited for his brother-in-law, though he didn't want the delay. Who knew what kind of flight he could get out of Gunnison or Montrose, both smaller airports. It was a five hour drive to Denver. "Are Haley and Taz coming in today?" he asked.

"Yeah. They're flying into Gunnison on Tuck's plane."

Isaac smiled. "All the ladies coming with them to get ready for the big day?"

"Yep. More of their friends will be rolling in Wednesday."

"Haley's so weird wanting to get married on a Thursday."

Cal smirked. "She wants to marry me. We can get married anywhere, anytime she wants."

Isaac shook his head, still a little shocked that his sister was getting married, but his brother-in-law was a great guy and treated Haley and Taz fabulous.

"Hey, Tuck and I browsed through your shop last night." Cal folded his arms across his chest.

"Okay." His stomach rolled a bit. He didn't need anyone's approval, but he looked up to Cal and Tucker.

"He loves your work. Like, wants you to sign autographs kind of loves."

Tuck was a really laidback, non-excitable guy. His wife on the other hand, Haley's friend, Maryn, was bouncing-off-the-walls-hilarious, and talked enough to make up for the two of them. Tuck's admiration meant a lot. "Um, thanks."

"We want to invest in you."

Isaac straightened, blinking. "Come again?"

"We both think you should be doing metal work full time." He paused, waiting, gauging Isaac's expression.

Isaac swallowed and admitted, "That's the dream."

"I thought so. Why didn't you just ask me?"

"That's not the way I work." Isaac shrugged, not liking the perceptive way Cal was studying him.

"I get ya." Cal nodded. "Write me up a business plan. I'm thinking your own land and shop, hire someone to clean, ship, do the paperwork. We'll find the right people for marketing and accounting. Oh, and Tuck also liked the idea of finding some high school or college kids to apprentice with you so we can grow it beyond what you can produce."

Isaac knew his mouth was hanging open. Every dream he'd had, and more, right in front of him. "You ... Tuck ..." He shook his head, hoping to clear it. "I'm not a charity case, Cal."

"Didn't say you were. We'll make back what we've invested in you and more." Cal slapped him on the shoulder. "Get the business plan to me and we'll crunch some numbers. I'm excited about this, so don't even think about talking me out of it."

Isaac barely resisted grabbing Cal in a bear hug, afraid a tear might spill if he didn't close his eyes tight. After a couple of slow breaths, he focused in on his future brother-in-law. "Thanks, man. This means a lot."

"It's going to be great." Cal cleared his throat. "I'm going to meet Haley at the airport. You want to come?"

"I'll drive with you. I'm hoping Gunnison will have a flight to Chicago so I don't have to drive to Montrose or Denver."

"Chicago?" Cal's brow wrinkled and his blue eyes were much too penetrating. "MacKenzie?"

"Left this morning," Isaac grunted out. The joy over this new business prospect dimmed as MacKenzie being gone washed over him again.

"She's coming back."

"She said she'd be back for the wedding, but, I need to, well, you know."

Cal nodded. "I do. Been there, buddy. Hurry and pack. You can take Tuck's plane to Chicago and it'll wait there for you and MacKenzie to come back."

"I can't." He shook his head and a strangled laugh escaped. "Just take Tucker's plane. You're joking, right?"

"We're partners now, bro. Tuck would agree with me."

"Agree with what?" A low, almost grumbly voice came from behind Isaac.

"Isaac needs your pilot to fly him to Chicago and pick up MacKenzie."

Tucker considered Isaac for a few seconds and must've seen the desperation written on his face. "Sounds great. Let's go."

Beck pulled up in a Lexus sport utility.

"Go, pack. We'll wait for you," Cal said.

"Not waiting too long," Beck called out of the open window. "I'm missing my girl."

Isaac jogged for his trailer. These men were handing out incredible opportunities like Tic Tacs and in a few hours he'd see MacKenzie. No one was going to be waiting on him.

CHAPTER SIXTEEN

MacKenzie had called ahead on Klein's phone and her parents were waiting for her at the airport Monday morning. Her sisters were both at work so she'd have to catch up with them tonight. Her dad drove her to her apartment. There was a lot of crying and retelling of every detail. She made the mistake of saying too much about Isaac. Her dad was scowling as her mom beamed.

"When do we get to meet this boy?" her mom asked.

"Yeah, when?" Her dad punched a freckled right fist into his large left palm.

MacKenzie laughed. "Maybe after I go back for the wedding. It's not like we have some commitment. I just like him." A lot.

"We'll see if you like him after I meet him," her dad grumbled, but MacKenzie could tell it was for show.

She hugged them both and promised to visit before she flew back to Crested Butte on Wednesday for the Thursday wedding. After they left she wandered around her apartment. It didn't feel like her spot anymore. She'd lived alone for years, but she didn't want to be alone right now. She changed into workout clothes and ran the mile and a half through the humidity to the gym. Crested Butte and cooler weather as she hiked through gorgeous terrain with Isaac seemed very far away. Her training group met at the gym most afternoons after work, so hopefully they'd be here.

She walked in and the front desk girl squealed, "MacKenzie. You're back! Are you okay? We heard you died or something."

MacKenzie forced a laugh. *Or something.* "I'm still alive."

"I'm so glad!"

"Thanks. Is any of the group here?"

"Peter and Lexi."

"Okay. Thanks. Good to see you."

"You too."

MacKenzie made her way to the training room, relieved that Vince wasn't here. She'd never appreciated his extra touchiness, but after having Isaac touch her, she knew she'd be even more repelled by Vince. He was a nice guy so she hated to be mean and tell him to back off, but she needed to soon. It wasn't fair to him when all she could think about was Isaac and was already counting down—two more days and she'd be back in Crested Butte. Hopefully Isaac wouldn't be upset that she left, but he should understand that she needed to see her parents and friends.

Peter and Lexi were all hugs, exclamations, and grins when MacKenzie walked in. She finally got them to settle down enough to work with her on some strength training. She hadn't done anything but hike since she'd been gone and didn't want to lose her strength. They were doing dead lifts when the door opened. MacKenzie dropped the weighted bar and whipped around. For one insane moment, she thought the tall, broad, dark-haired man was Isaac, then he came out of the shadows.

"MacKenzie," Vince whispered her name almost reverently. He hurried across the floor and stopped in front of her. "I thought you were dead. The police said you were missing. Are you okay?"

MacKenzie was touched by the sincerity in his handsome face and grateful he hadn't grabbed her or anything.

"I'm okay. Crazy, scary story, but I'm excited to move past it and get back to life." Life meaning hurrying back to Crested Butte to determine if anything was going to happen with her and Isaac.

"I'm all for getting back to life." Vince grinned, wrapped his arms around her, and whipped her off of her feet.

"Vince," she protested.

He whirled her around like she was the prize at the fair then pulled her in and pressed a kiss to her lips. The door slammed. MacKenzie had no clue if someone had come in or left. She only knew she had to stop this now.

She used all of her strength to strong arm him away from her.

117

"Vince. Stop."

He pulled back and she took a huge step away. Peter and Lexi were watching the two of them with unabashed interest.

"I met someone."

Vince's eyebrows dipped together and Peter and Lexi took a step closer.

"I'm sorry. I don't know if you meant anything by that kiss, but I met someone who I am very interested in and I ..." This was getting uncomfortable, especially with the scowl on Vince's face. Was she assuming too much or not enough? "I'm going back to Colorado to be with him in a couple of days."

Lexi lit up. "You *have* to tell us the story."

Peter nodded his agreement. They all looked to Vince. His shoulders slowly relaxed. "I'm sorry, Kenzie. I always kind of hoped."

"I know." She wished she could lie to spare his feelings and say she'd hoped for something too, but she wasn't going to lie again, ever. "But I really fell hard for Isaac."

They all gathered around and forgot about strength training for a while as MacKenzie shared her story of the past few weeks. Reliving it again was both terrifying and wonderful. Her longing for Isaac kept growing and growing. She hoped she could make it through the next few days so she could be with him again.

* * *

Isaac exited the plane later that afternoon with MacKenzie's apartment address programmed in his phone and a growing hope in his heart. He was going to see her soon. How would she react? He was more nervous than a first-time bull rider.

He used the Uber app and within minutes a driver had picked him up and they were cruising toward MacKenzie's apartment. Tucker's pilot had told him he'd refuel and wait until Isaac told him if they were going back tonight or tomorrow. The pilot said it was no worry and just to keep him informed. What a crazy life his brother-in-law and friends lived. To have a jet and a pilot at your disposal? Isaac didn't know that he'd ever have that kind of money, but that was fine. The thought of finally being able to go full time with his business was enough for him.

He arrived at MacKenzie's apartment. It was nice, just a little north of downtown. She had a doorman who welcomed him in and asked who he wanted to visit.

"MacKenzie Gunthrie," his voice felt raw and he swallowed hard.

"Oh, our sweet MacKenzie. You just missed her, young man. Can I leave her a message?"

Isaac's shoulders fell. He'd missed her. Haley had given him MacKenzie's cell number. Would she have her cell back after all she'd gone through or would the FBI have it? "Do you know where she's gone?"

"Ah. I can't give out information like that."

Isaac nodded. "Of course. Sorry. I'll check back in a little while."

"Did you come from far away, son?"

"Just flew in from Colorado."

"To see MacKenzie?" A bushy white eyebrow rose.

"Yes. She's been staying at my family's ranch the past few weeks."

"Are you Isaac?"

He jolted. "Yes."

The older man smiled. "That girl's a spot of sunshine for me. She told me a bit about what happened and how Isaac saved her."

Isaac's heart picked up. She'd talked about him with her doorman. That had to mean something.

"Now, I'm not saying where she is, but she was wearing some of those spandex clothes."

Isaac smiled at the thought of seeing MacKenzie in spandex.

"And she really likes to train for those Spartan races at some gym called Reach. Corner of Chicago Avenue and Paulina," he whispered out of the side of his mouth.

"Thank you." Isaac wanted to hug the old man. He settled for a hand shake then he hurried out of the door and put the address and gym name into his phone. A mile and a half. He should get another Uber, but he set off on foot instead. He could probably beat an Uber, the way he was soaring. He made it to the gym and was sweating from the humidity. He was accustomed to Crested Butte's cooler temperatures. The air conditioned interior was a relief.

A young blonde perched over the front desk. "Can I help you?" Her eyes trailed over him as her tongue trailed over her lips. Oh, no.

"I'm here to see MacKenzie Gunthrie."

"Really?" Her unnaturally dark eyebrows arched up. "Why?"

"Can you please tell me where she is?"

"Sure, honey, I'll tell you whatever you want."

Isaac waited. "MacKenzie?" he asked again.

The girl pointed, red lips pouting from him obviously not taking the bait. "Through that door is where they train for Spartan."

"Thanks." He gave her a genuine smile and she sighed dreamily. Isaac turned and hurried for the door before she got any ideas. He swung it open to see MacKenzie being whirled in some dude's arms. The guy lowered her to him and kissed her. Isaac's heart stopped. No. MacKenzie had a boyfriend. No! Why hadn't she told him?

He let the door fall closed and turned, slowly making his way back past the receptionist. "Did you find her?"

He shook his head, unable to talk, and walked back into the oppressive air. Something inside begged him to wait and talk to MacKenzie, but he couldn't handle seeing her with that guy. Isaac had assumed she was unattached and had fallen for him and only him. The fact of the matter was she'd been scared and Isaac had been there. He didn't think MacKenzie was the type for casual relationships, but that was another stupid assumption. Isaac had told her he loved her and she hadn't responded. She obviously had a boyfriend and at the first opportunity had flown back to Chicago to be with him.

Isaac texted the pilot that he wanted to fly back to Colorado as soon as possible then ordered another Uber. He officially decided that he hated Chicago and would never come back again.

CHAPTER SEVENTEEN

The next two days were busy for Isaac, and luckily everyone else was too distracted to bug him much about where MacKenzie was. He helped Haley and Cal with wedding prep, found a piece of property, and set up a temporary shop for his business. Things went fast when you paid in cash. The property he bought was north of the ski resorts in a valley below the tiny town of Gothic. Isaac liked the isolation and the beauty of the area.

His thoughts were on MacKenzie far too much. He wondered if she'd come back for the wedding and what he would say to her if she did. His chest hurt every time he pictured her in that guy's arms.

He turned off the welder and stared across his shop out the open door. All was quiet as everyone else had gone to sleep for the night. The crickets chirping and the wind rushing through the aspen trees outside weren't enough distraction to forget about MacKenzie.

"So, you're excited to ditch me, eh?"

Isaac straightened at the sound of his father's voice. He pulled off his apron and helmet and sighed. "I'm not excited to ditch you, but to get on with my dreams."

"Don't lie to me, boy. You're excited to ditch me." His dad gave him half a smile. "I think the Sundstrom boy will work out well on the ranch."

"Me too. You'll be fine without me."

"Yeah, but I'll miss you."

Isaac's head flew up as his dad's gaze skittered away. His dad was mush with Haley and Taz, but Isaac wondered half the time if the man even liked his own son. He cleared his throat. "I won't be too far away."

His dad nodded and fingered a metal floral arrangement. "It's impressive work you're doing, son."

Isaac swallowed hard, not sure if he'd heard right. "Thank you, sir."

"I'm, well, I'm sorry." His dad was looking everywhere but at Isaac. "I know I haven't been supportive of you, and thank the good Lord, Cal is a better man than me and saw how talented you are and … I was scared, okay?"

Isaac took a step closer, wanting to hug his dad, which was just awkward. They hadn't hugged since the brief, uncomfortable moment at his mom's graveside when everyone was watching and it was expected they embrace. "Scared of what?" he asked in a low tone.

"You failing and it breaking your heart. I've never seen you so passionate about anything, besides MacKenzie, that is." His dad flashed him a mischievous grin.

Isaac ignored the last part, though his heart dinged with the pain. "You thought I would fail?"

"No." His dad shook his head. "No, but I worried, that's what parents do, and without your mom here to mediate between us. I don't know how to talk to you very well. Never have."

Now that was the truth. His mom always smoothed over their fights and helped them see the best in each other. Haley had done a pretty good job of it too, but with both women gone their relationship was tough.

"Thanks, Dad."

"For what?" His dad rolled his eyes. "All I tried to do was hold you back."

Isaac chuckled. "Thanks for admitting it."

His dad strode forward, took his hand in a firm grip then pounded him on the shoulder. "I'm right proud of you, boy."

Before Isaac could respond, his dad ripped his hand away and hurried out of the shop. Isaac savored it for a while. The only time his dad had ever been proud of him was when he'd sacked the quarterback in the state championship football game and the Titans had kept the lead and won the game. He put his tools away slowly. Things were good in his life. If only he didn't have this hole from missing MacKenzie.

CHAPTER EIGHTEEN

MacKenzie was in turmoil as she drove into Crested Butte in a rental car. The short flight to Denver and then onto Gunnison hadn't given her enough time to think, or maybe it'd given her too much. She'd had a great time being with friends and family in Chicago, but it was like she couldn't get back to Crested Butte, or more accurately, Isaac, quick enough.

She'd gotten her cell back from the FBI Monday night and had immediately texted Haley for Isaac's number. He didn't answer when she called and his voice mail was an automatic recitation of the number instead of his voice, but she'd left a lengthy message telling him she was sorry she'd left and couldn't wait to see him again on Wednesday. She'd said love you before her goodbye without really meaning to let those words escape. His lack of response to her message was killing her. She'd wanted to text or call him again, but forced herself to wait.

She was ready to make a leap for him and had been tempted to start looking for teaching jobs in Crested Butte or somewhere close like Gunnison. Maybe she could move there for a while and run Haley's store, if Haley wasn't ticked at her for leaving the store closed the past few days. She hated to leave her family, training partners, and students, but she needed to know if something could develop with Isaac. She'd never felt like this about anyone.

Her heart was beating a staccato as she pulled off the main road and into the ranch yard. She searched for Isaac's truck, her hope deflating when she didn't spot it. Unsure where to go, she pulled up to Trevor's house, climbed slowly out and stretched. The place looked deserted. Where was everybody? Most of her girl's camp friends should be here and Isaac should be here, waiting, excited to see her, ready to pick her up in his arms, spin her around, and kiss her.

She knocked on every door—Trevor's, Haley's, Isaac's. She poked around the barn and Isaac's shop. All of his metal art and most of his welding supplies were gone. What did that mean? Had he finally found his own spot? In two days?

Pulling out her cell phone, she dialed Haley's number. It went straight to voice mail. Well, her wedding day was tomorrow. Maybe she was a bit busy. She tried Maryn next.

"Hello?" Maryn sounded cautious, completely unlike herself.

"Maryn, it's MacKenzie."

"Kenzie!" Maryn shrieked. "Where are you? Get your skinny bum over here."

"Over where?"

"Haley's getting married in an hour."

"The wedding's tomorrow." MacKenzie's grip tightened on the phone. In an hour? She needed to change and find Isaac, and she'd been no help to her friend who had saved her this past few weeks.

"You been under a rock girl? The media went crazy with your story and tied it all into Crested Butte, Haley, and Cal. Someone in town must've leaked the wedding tomorrow evening so we changed it. Everyone was here and we knew you were on your way today. So she's having an afternoon wedding that only close friends and the locals know about. Up in some beautiful valley above the ski resort. Go to Cal's hotel and they'll shuttle you up here. You know the way?"

"Yeah." MacKenzie rushed for her car. She'd have to change and fix up her hair at the resort.

"Kay. Get here quick. Love ya."

"You too."

MacKenzie drove like a wild woman, hoping all the police were at the wedding and wouldn't pull her over. At least now she had a driver's license. It felt good to be safe and legal again.

The resort exterior was vertical plank boards, huge timbers, and lots of windows. She grabbed her overnight bag and her dress bag and left her car with the valet.

The front desk clerk was a good-looking twenty-something kid.

"Hi. I'm here for Haley Turnbow's wedding."

"Name please." He gave her a toothy smile.

"MacKenzie Gunthrie."

His eyebrows shot up. "Girl! Everyone has been waiting for you." He pulled out a packet. "Here's your room key. Get on up there and change and I'll get the Jeep ready to take you up."

"Thank you." Her bottom lip quivered. They were waiting for her. Why hadn't they called her to let her know the wedding had been changed then? Just an oversight or was everyone upset at her for leaving like she did?

She took the stairs to save time and found her suite on the third floor. It was gorgeous: rustic wood, warm leather, and modern stainless steel combined to a homey feel. The picture windows overlooked the valley below. Changing quickly into her teal-colored knee-length gauzy dress, she hoped everything was okay with her and Isaac. She touched up her makeup and ran some serum through her hair to try to make it shine and the curls lay a little better.

As she descended the stairs, she prayed that Isaac would be happy to see her. She'd missed him so much. What if he didn't feel the same? The front desk guy ushered her into a Jeep and the driver greeted her then drove quickly up the mountain.

The valley was like an outdoor landscape painting. A grassy area butted up against the mountainside with its cascade of pine trees. There was a huge canopy stretching from tree to tree to ensure the wedding party was shaded, but it was all open so the backdrop was just the beautiful outdoors. The tables and chairs were decorated with white, teal, and orange with floral accents. Everything was outdoorsy looking but also very professionally done.

She spotted Isaac standing up front with Cal and Tucker. Isaac looked so breathtakingly handsome in a dark gray suit and teal tie. His green eyes met hers and the scenery and people fell away. She saw him mouth, "Mac."

MacKenzie grinned and started toward him when she heard someone calling her name in a sort of hushed yell, "Kenzie, Kenzie!"

Tearing her gaze from Isaac, she whirled around. Maryn was rushing toward her, her blonde curls bouncing. "Kenzie, the wedding's about to start! What are you *doing*?"

"I, Isaac."

"You're going to have to talk to him after. Come sit with the girls."

Maryn took her arm and led her to the group. Alyssa and Beck. Holly and Jordan. Erin and Matt. Nikki and Darrin. Lindsey was the only other friend without a handsome husband. She wondered where Kynley and Summer were. Nobody had heard from Trin in years. Her group of friends were gorgeous people. Like a bunch of Hollywood A-listers. No wonder the paparazzi wanted to get the scoop on this wedding. All of her married friends but Erin had married extreme wealth and had been in the tabloids at different times.

She glanced at Isaac again. If she had her way, she wouldn't marry a wealthy man. She would have to humiliate herself and sing the Camp Wallakee song at her wedding. That was just fine with her. Isaac was more than worth it.

Maryn squeezed in next to Alyssa and pulled Kenzie down with her. The wedding march started and they all stood before she had a chance to do more than whisper hello to everyone. Usually, she'd be dying to talk to her friends, but all she wanted right now was Isaac.

Taz walked importantly down the aisle in front of his mom and grandpa. Taz was adorable in his little suit with his dark curls and his broad smile, missing his two bottom teeth. Haley was exquisite in the most gorgeous dress MacKenzie had seen. It was white satin and off-white lace with teal ribbon woven around the waist. With her dark hair and green eyes she was an unbelievably pretty bride.

MacKenzie glanced back at Isaac, noticing Cal staring with a look of pure joy at Haley. She wished Isaac was looking at her like that, but his eyes were hooded and his smile looked practiced. What was going on?

The wedding ceremony was sweet and not too long. MacKenzie should've paid better attention, but all she could think about was getting to Isaac. After the ceremony was over, Cal and Haley shared a really long kiss until Taz said, "Stop! My turn!"

They'd broken apart with a laugh to hug and kiss their son and walk together as a family down the aisle. Taz perched in Cal's right arm while Cal held Haley close with his left. MacKenzie felt bad that she was so caught up in her selfish desires to hug and kiss Isaac that she hadn't really shared in their family joy. They were adorable and so happy. They all deserved it. These might be her future in-laws. Her stomach leaped. Oh, she hoped so.

The wedding party moved to an area set up next to the towering cake to receive congratulations. Caterers were arranging a buffet that smelled delectable, but MacKenzie knew she couldn't eat a bite until she worked things out with Isaac. The Camp Wallakee group all stood and everyone started talking at once, trying to catch up, and firing questions at MacKenzie about what in the world had happened and why hadn't she called them? What made Haley so special? She knew they were teasing, but wanted to tell them they should be grateful she didn't involve them.

MacKenzie loved her friends and was literally and figuratively wrapped in a big hug by all of them, but she kept looking for Isaac. Maryn asked when MacKenzie was going to marry her own billionaire hunk. She reddened and almost told her she wanted a humble hunk who did metal art, but she didn't know if he wanted her. Where had he disappeared to and why did she have this awful feeling that he wasn't searching for her like she was for him?

* * *

Isaac had almost given up hope that MacKenzie was coming to the wedding. Maybe hope was the wrong word. He wanted to see her so badly he ached, but at the same time he didn't want to face her. She had a boyfriend back in Chicago and had probably just turned to Isaac the past few weeks because of how afraid she was and how much Isaac had pushed her to be with him. He assumed she'd been reluctant to

127

date him because of Brad or the crime lord being after her, the thought of a boyfriend hadn't even crossed his mind. He probably should've asked more questions and kissed less. Oh, kissing, Mac. He'd never get the privilege again.

It was good she was here. If she hadn't made it to the wedding it would've been his fault. Haley had been running around like a crazy woman when they decided to move the event up a day to hopefully escape the paparazzi feasting on their happiness. She'd thrust her phone at Isaac. "Call Kenzie for me and make sure she knows about the change of plans." She'd rushed on without his response and he'd just stared at MacKenzie's contact information and her picture from Facebook for long minutes then put the phone back in Haley's purse.

When MacKenzie walked into the canopy, her long, dark hair cascading around her shoulders, her curves highlighted in the teal dress, and her dark eyes searching for him, he started toward her. Cal had grabbed his arm and said something like, "Dude. You're going to have to wait."

Isaac restrained himself, but didn't take his eyes off her. When she finally met his gaze, her name had come out in a croak of wanting, "Mac." Cal had shaken his head, but didn't say anything.

Isaac forced himself to stop staring at MacKenzie and try to enjoy this moment for his sister, nephew, and new brother-in-law. Their happiness made him happy. He was okay. Maybe he'd never have this for himself, but his family was what mattered. He needed to put his selfish desires for MacKenzie aside and concentrate on making Haley's day the best day possible.

As soon as the wedding was over he went around the opposite side of the aisle to avoid MacKenzie and was one of the first to congratulate the new family.

Taz laughed when he picked him up and squeezed him. "Love ya, Uncle Isaac."

"You too, bud."

"Did ya see the pretty ladies over there?" Taz asked, nodding his head like a suave teenager. "New girlfriends."

Isaac chuckled and followed his gaze to Haley's group of girl's camp friends. They were all surrounding MacKenzie and he could stare at her for a few seconds without her knowing. She was so beautiful. "Good luck, little man."

Taz laughed like a little maniac. "Maybe I'll marry them."

Cal laughed, took Isaac's outstretched hand and pulled him into a hug with Taz between them. "You need to wait a few years, son. Isaac on the other hand needs to go talk to 'Mac'."

Isaac shifted uncomfortably and set Taz down so his nephew could greet the teenage girls waiting in line for a chance to hug their little boyfriend.

"You heard that?" he asked Cal.

"Heard what?" Haley finished talking to an older couple and turned to him.

Isaac enveloped her in his arms. "Nothing. You look gorgeous, sis. Love you."

She beamed up at him. "Love you too."

People were crowding from behind so he let his sister go and turned away. He'd make himself useful and go check if the caterers needed any help. It was in the opposite direction of MacKenzie so that was good. He knew he couldn't avoid her all afternoon, but he needed more time before she saw how she'd broken him. He didn't want her compassion. He wanted her to dump her boyfriend and move to Crested Butte. That wasn't going to happen, so he'd just have to survive until she disappeared and he could bury himself in his work.

* * *

MacKenzie was ushered along with her group of friends to congratulate the newlyweds. Taz kept calling Maryn his girlfriend, much to Tucker's protest. Taz studied Maryn and Tucker for a few seconds then said sorrowfully, "I'm sorry. You can't be my girlfriend anymore, you gots to be a wife."

Cal roared with laughter. "Well, at least he's learned some

boundaries."

Maryn pointed at MacKenzie. "Maybe Kenzie can be your new girlfriend."

Taz looked her over then winked. "Oh, yes, yes, *yes*."

The entire group was laughing now. MacKenzie thought Taz resembled his uncle far too much. She only wished Isaac was as insistent that she be his girlfriend.

Taz slyly cocked his head and said to Tucker, "Do you have respect for me now?"

"Oh my goodness!" Maryn shook her head. "I love you, little man."

"You can't love me, you're a wife."

Most of the group had already congratulated the happy couple. Taz gave MacKenzie a hug around the waist then moved on to flirt with Lindsey. Cal wrapped a strong arm around MacKenzie. "How are you? We haven't seen you since that crazy night."

"I'm doing good."

"Did Isaac track you down?"

"Not yet."

Cal eyed her strangely. "Oh?"

Haley reached out to hug MacKenzie. "Where is that big lug?" Haley asked.

MacKenzie didn't want to get into Isaac right now. Where was he? Why hadn't he responded to her phone message? She was so nervous to talk to him, but wanted it to happen right now at the same time.

"Congrats," she said to Haley. "You are absolutely gorgeous!" She hugged her friend tight. "Love you."

"Love you too, but I want to talk about *you* and Isaac."

"Not today." MacKenzie moved on so Lindsey could gush over Haley's dress.

Maryn squeezed her hand. "We're going to find a table for dinner."

"Okay. I'll be right there after I find a restroom." Were there even restrooms in this remote location?

"I'll come with you."

"No. Sorry. I … need a minute."

Maryn eyed her for a second, but then it clicked and her eyes widened. "Gotcha."

Tucker nodded to MacKenzie and pulled his tiny wife close. They were so cute. Beckham and Alyssa were just ahead and it was fun to see Alyssa's rounded belly. She'd be the second of them to be a mom. Crazy and so exciting.

MacKenzie walked away, but she couldn't care less about a bathroom, she had to find Isaac. She glimpsed his dark, curly hair over by where the caterers were setting up. Hurrying that direction, she could see his face now. Oh, how she longed to run her fingers down his smooth cheek. He turned and his green eyes lit up as they met hers, but then they dimmed and he turned away and took off.

What was going on? She was the runner, not him. Isaac was the stand up and fight kind of guy, and until the past two days he'd been the guy that was fighting for her.

MacKenzie was confused, hurt, and not going to lie down and let him kick her to the curb. She hurried after him. He headed off into the trees and was almost hidden by a grove of aspen trees. He was honestly running from her.

"Isaac, stop!" she hollered out, running in heels was not conducive to a chase.

He stopped and turned. The shadows of the trees hid his expression as she approached. When she finally glimpsed his face he looked so sad. "Hey," he muttered. "I was going to … get something for Haley."

"In the forest?"

"Yep. If you'll excuse me." He started to turn away.

MacKenzie grabbed his arm, even through his suit coat she could feel the tense muscles in his forearm. What was going on? "No, I won't excuse you. I haven't seen you in two days and I wanted to say hi."

A muscle clenched in his jaw. His green eyes darkened and narrowed. "Hi," he ground out.

"You're mad at me?" She dropped his arm and stepped back. "I'm sorry I ran off without saying goodbye. It was really early in the morning and the FBI said it was now or never and I felt like that was my opportunity to go see my parents. This whole deal was really hard on them."

His face softened. "I understand, MacKenzie, and you had every right to go see your parents."

She flinched at the use of her full name. "Why didn't you return my call?"

"What call?" He took a step closer to her.

"I left a voice mail on your phone." She bit at the inside of her cheek. Had he not heard the message, or was he embarrassed because she'd said she loved him?

"I never got it."

MacKenzie pulled her phone out of her bra. Isaac blushed and looked away. She pressed a few buttons then showed him. "See, here's your number. 970-880-9771."

He shook his head. "My number's 9770."

"Haley." MacKenzie groaned. "She has had a lot going on."

Isaac smiled sadly at her. "I appreciate you calling, MacKenzie, but—"

"You call me Mac," she interrupted him.

He licked his lips and his eyes roved over her face. "I can't."

"Why not?"

His Adam's apple bobbed before he said in such a low voice she had to lean closer to understand, "If I had you for a girlfriend, I wouldn't want another man kissing you and calling you nicknames." He clenched and unclenched his fist.

"What?" She was so confused. "I thought *you* were my boyfriend." Her face flared. The way he was acting he obviously didn't want her for a girlfriend.

"Really?" His eyebrows shot up and a furrow appeared between his eyes. "Maybe you should tell that to the guy you were kissing at the gym."

"Kissing at what gym? Who was I kissing?" Isaac was maddening. Why was he making up some story about her kissing some guy? Did he need an excuse to get away from her?

"I don't know." He pushed a hand through his hair, mussing the curls that had been sculpted to perfection for the wedding. "Some dark-haired guy with lots of fake muscles."

"Fake muscles? Vince?" Vince had kissed her, but she'd told him not to and hadn't returned his kiss. "How did you…" Her voice trailed off and his anger and distance and Cal asking if Isaac "found her" and her doorman's confusing story about someone named Isaac stopping by all suddenly made sense. "You came to Chicago?"

He nodded tersely.

"You came to Chicago!" He did care. He cared a lot. MacKenzie threw herself at him.

He remained stiff and didn't wrap his arms around her. "I'm not into two-timers, MacKenzie."

MacKenzie stepped back, hating that her voice trembled as she spoke, "You call me *Mac* and I'm not a two-timer."

He looked so sad. "I saw you. I saw you kissing him."

"No, you didn't. Vince picked me up and kissed me then I cussed him out and told him and my other friends all about you." She slapped her hand on his chest. *Oh, my, those muscles are nicely formed. Don't get distracted.* "You want to call Vince and ask him about it?"

He looked away. "No. It's okay."

MacKenzie pushed the number on her phone. Vince answered on the first ring and she didn't waste any time putting it on speaker. "Vince. When you kissed me on Monday how did I react?"

"You told me not to and told me about your boyfriend in Colorado. Why?"

MacKenzie studied Isaac's face. The confusion melted away and he stared at her with a hunger that was undeniable.

"Thanks." MacKenzie ended the call and stored the phone in her bra again.

Isaac studied her for a few seconds then reached out and took both of her hands in his. "I was so dumb. I left as soon as I saw him kiss you."

MacKenzie thought back. "I remember hearing a door close."

He nodded.

MacKenzie squeezed his hands. "All I've been thinking about is you, wanting to get back to you and see if what we have is worth me relocating for."

Isaac caught a breath. "You'd relocate, for me?"

"Yes."

He tugged her a little bit closer. "I'm sorry I reacted so badly. I told you I loved you and then you were gone and I came after you to show you how I felt and saw him holding you."

"What crappy timing you have, my love." She stood on tiptoes and pressed her lips to his.

Isaac released her hands and wrapped his arms around her back. "Horrible timing." He lowered his head and took his time kissing her until she was breathless and the world was spinning.

"Did you mean it?" she asked.

"What?" he whispered.

"When you said you loved me." She lowered her gaze. "I thought it might've just been a reaction to an intense situation."

Isaac gently tilted her chin up with his thumb. "It was a reaction … to you. I love how brave and strong you are." He kissed her softly. "I love how beautiful and kind you are." He kissed her again. "I love every part of you." His voice lowered to a husky moan, "Mac."

MacKenzie grinned and kissed him back.

CHAPTER NINETEEN

MacKenzie sealed the huge cardboard box with packaging tape and then attached the label she'd just printed. Large arms wrapped around her waist and pulled her against her favorite chest in the world. Isaac nuzzled her neck with his lips. "All ready to ship?"

"Yep. UPS should be here any minute."

He spun her around and kissed her for several wonderful seconds. "I feel bad that you're working as a grunt when you should be teaching school."

MacKenzie laughed. "I'll be teaching soon enough." The school board had all but promised her a position as the third grade teacher when Mrs. Campbell had her baby in January. "Besides, I'd rather be with you."

Isaac smelled like metal, fire, and his musky cologne. MacKenzie loved it. She loved him.

"This has been a dream come true," he said. "Cal and Tuck backing me. The shop and property. The business taking off. Most of all being with you."

She smiled.

He took her hand. "C'mere, I wanted to show you something."

They walked out into the crisp fall air. It was definitely cooler in Crested Butte, but it was so beautiful and she was with Isaac. She'd take him over warm weather any time. An excavator slowly crested the rise. A couple of trucks followed behind it.

MacKenzie glanced at Isaac. "What's this?"

Isaac grinned and dropped to his knee. He pulled out a ring box and MacKenzie covered her mouth with her hands.

"I wanted to have the house started before I begged you to be my wife."

MacKenzie couldn't find any words.

135

"Mac?" Isaac opened the ring box to reveal a thick white gold band set with a large princess cut diamond. "Will you marry me?"

MacKenzie threw herself at him and knocked him over onto his rear. Isaac laughed and hugged her there in the dirt. "Is that a yes?"

"Can I ride on the back of your tandem bike?"

Isaac's green eyes swept over her with warmth. "You like that Crested Butte tradition?"

MacKenzie ducked her head and admitted, "I've been daydreaming about riding on the back of your tandem bike for far too long."

He pulled her close. "I would love to have you on the back of my bike." He arched his eyebrows. "So, it's a yes?"

"Oh, yes!" She kissed him fervently.

Men piled out of the construction vehicles and stood watching them. Someone yelled, "Wow, Isaac, guess she said yes?"

MacKenzie glanced around. The loud redhead guy who'd hit on her at Long Lake was grinning from the steps of an excavator. He tipped his hard hat to her.

"How did they know?" MacKenzie asked.

"Everyone but you knew, my love."

"Of course the fiancée is the last to know."

"No secrets in this town. Taz told everyone he was going to lose another girlfriend."

MacKenzie laughed. "Give me that dang ring already so nobody else tries to make me their girlfriend."

"No one had better try," Isaac growled.

He slid the ring on her finger and she kissed him. Isaac lifted her off the ground. "Shall we supervise the building of your dream house, Mrs. Turnbow?"

"Give me a pretty ring, build me a house, and think you can call me whatever you want?"

"What would you prefer I call you?" His green eyes did that snake charmer thing again. She wanted to tell him he could call her whatever he wanted because she was his.

"Mac," she managed to say breathlessly.

Isaac grinned and swooped her into his arms. "I love you, Mac," he shouted for everyone to hear.

The construction guys chuckled and left them alone. It was much later when they finally started supervising the building of their dream home.

ADDITIONAL WORKS

By Cami Checketts

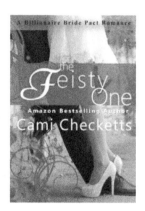 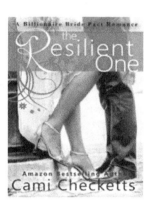 

Also available:

Caribbean Rescue: Destination Billionaire Romance
Shadows in the Curtain: Destination Billionaire Romance
Protect This
Blog This
Redeem This
Oh, Come on Be Faithful
The Broken Path
Dead Running
Dying to Run
Christmas Kisses: An Echo Ridge Anthology
Full Court Devotion: Christmas in Snow Valley

ABOUT THE AUTHOR

Cami is a part-time author, part-time exercise consultant, part-time housekeeper, full-time wife, and overtime mother of four adorable boys. Sleep and relaxation are fond memories. She's never been happier.

Sign up for Cami's newsletter to receive a free ebook and information about new releases, discounts, and promotions here.

If you enjoyed *The Protective One,* please consider posting a review on Amazon, Goodreads, or your personal blog. Thank you for helping to spread the word.

www.camichecketts.com

The Rebellious One by Jeanette Lewis

The Billionaire Bride Pact

"I, Holly Frances Clarke, do solemnly swear, that someday
I'll marry a billionaire ...
OR I will have to sing the Camp Wallakee song
(with the bird calls) at my wedding."

CHAPTER 1

THE DIAMOND RING WAS RIDICULOUSLY LARGE, even by Holly's
standards. She liked blingy jewelry as much as the next girl, and when
it came time to pick an engagement ring, she'd steered Brit toward
Grace Kelly's famous ten-carat diamond. Holly's seven-carat stone
wasn't quite as big as Grace's, but it was the same emerald cut and it
did have the same diamond baguettes inset on either side.

She'd hoped Brit would be *inspired* by Grace Kelly's ring. Turns
out there was such a thing as too literal a translation.

There was a slight hissing sound and Holly looked up, directly
into her mother's frosty stare. Surprised, she scanned the banquet
table, where the rest of the ladies who made up Le Ciel resort's
charitable planning committee had lapsed into silence. Holly looked
back in time to see her mother's glance shifted to her left hand, and
Holly realized she was tapping the back of her engagement ring
against the table like a judge banging a gavel.

Oh.

"Sorry," Holly muttered. She clasped her hands together in her
lap.

Her mother gave her a practiced smile, then turned back to the discussion she was directing. "The executive chef told me today he's found enough squab for the seventh course after all. I was afraid we'd have to substitute with Cornish game hens, but he pulled some strings and they'll be flown in from Toronto the day before the party."

There was murmured approval at the news, and Holly's mother beamed. The brunch was the last planning meeting before Le Ciel's annual October ball to benefit the hospital, and as committee chairman, Frances Clarke was in her element.

Frances looked younger than her fifty-seven years, with an olive-tinged complexion and straight dark hair that she wore in layers, reminding Holly of a brunette Sharon Osbourne. A rigorous regime of yoga, juice cleanses, and healthy eating had helped her maintain a slim figure, and the regular Botox took care of any wrinkles that dared appear. She never left the house without full hair and makeup, and her designer closet was the envy of her social circle.

"Julia, did you speak to the videographer?" she asked.

Julia Higgins wore a ring with a chocolate diamond almost as big as Holly's. The stone flashed in the late morning sunlight as she tucked a strand of silvery hair behind her ear. "Yes, and they have a computer program to make the video look vintage. I don't know how it works, but he assured me it will look straight out of 1912 by the time he's finished." The theme this year was "A Night Aboard the *Titanic*," and the foundation would spare no expense to make the ball authentic.

The women fell silent as Frances consulted her agenda. Holly glanced around the table, where many of the Wastach Front's most influential families were represented. Some of the women were prominent in their own right, but most were here as representatives of their larger families, such as wives of politicians, business moguls, and sports stars, and heirs of family dynasties that had been running Utah for generations. All were impeccably dressed in designer suits or dresses, all with plentiful amounts of jewelry on display. They'd finished the main course and were nibbling delicately on the raspberry sorbet and lemon butter cookies provided by Le Ciel's catering.

"As you can see, the Barn is coming along." Frances waved her hand around the room. "The Barn" was the informal name for the primary reception center on Le Ciel resort—a world-class vacation destination that was owned and operated by Holly's family. Why it was called "the Barn" was anyone's guess, the place resembled more of a fort than a barn with its stone walls, high, timbered ceiling, and central courtyard. Sounds of construction drifted into the brunch from the huge main room, where workers were busy transforming the space into the *Titanic*.

"If you'd like to stop by and check on the progress throughout the week, you're more than welcome," Holly's mother continued. "Send me or Holly a text first so we can alert security. Are there any questions?"

Tanya Emery, wife of a respected Utah oncologist, raised her hand. "I think we might need to find one or two more activities. I'm afraid people won't stay for the auction if the only thing to do is dancing."

There was a pause as everyone considered this; then, the women all began talking at once. Most agreed with Tanya. From the general tone of barely contained hysteria around the table, Holly gathered this could be a catastrophe in the making.

"Ladies!" Frances raised her hands, and the women quieted instantly. "Let's not panic. We don't need anything too involved. We've all done our research; let's brainstorm another activity that would go with the theme."

The women immediately launched into chatter.

"Shuffleboard?"

"Cards?"

"What about a second- or third-class activity?"

"What else suggests '*Titanic*' to you?"

"The ice bucket challenge?" Holly said loudly.

Conversation screeched to a halt, and for the second time in less than twenty minutes, Holly was acutely aware of her mother's pinch-lipped stare.

"At least it would be historically accurate," Holly said. She tried to lighten her tone and turn it into a joke, but from the frowns around the table, she knew no one was buying it.

Frances continued as if she hadn't spoken. "Shuffleboard might be fun. We could set up a game area in one of the rooms across the courtyard."

The idea caught on and soon the committee buzzed with ideas for more period-specific games.

Finally, after making sure everyone knew their assignments, Frances dismissed the meeting. Chairs scraped against the hardwood floors as everyone rose. Some of the women made their way outside, but most lingered, obviously wanting a private word with Frances.

"Holly, wait," Frances ordered when Holly made a move to follow those who were leaving. Holly had no choice but to sink back into her chair. She answered emails on her phone while various women asked her mother for costume advice, her opinion on the seating chart, and even the recipe for today's lemon cookies. Frances handled them all with the decisive air of one who likes being in charge.

Finally the room cleared, and Holly was alone with her mother. "The ice bucket challenge?" Frances said, glaring at Holly. "That was extremely inappropriate."

"And throwing a *Titanic*-themed party isn't?" Holly said. "Over a thousand people *died*, mother."

"The charity ball is about raising money for a good cause, and the best way to do that is to generate excitement," Frances pointed out. "People identify with the *Titanic*; you heard how enthusiastic everyone was about their costumes."

Yes, Holly had heard. The entire first half of the brunch had been devoted to updates on custom-ordered dresses, included riveting topics such as what color each woman planned to wear, whether a dress copied Kate Winslet's costume from the movie too closely, and whether it was absolutely necessary to wear a corset to bring the look together—the women had decided it was.

Holly bit her lip. When they'd chosen the theme back in January, she'd been as excited as everyone else. She'd designed her own gown, and Genevieve, her costume maker, had done a superb job. Standing in front of Genevieve's three-way mirror at her final fitting last week, Holly had felt every inch a *Titanic*-era princess.

Le Ciel's charity ball had a long tradition, dating back as far as Holly could remember. As a child, she'd always kept a close eye on the preparations, and watching her mother get ready for the evening was a highlight every year. When she'd been old enough to start attending the ball herself, she'd had even more fun designing her costumes and watching Genevieve bring them to life. Her costume from last year's fairy tale ball, a replica of Giselle's turquoise dress from *Enchanted*, still hung in the closet of her spare bedroom.

Usually Holly couldn't wait for the party. So why did she feel so cynical about the whole thing this year?

"I'm sorry, mother," Holly finally said. "I guess I'm just tired and feeling overwhelmed."

Frances adjusted the hem of her gray Chanel suit jacket. "You need to make better use of your time … not to mention your help. There's a reason we hired Marion."

Marion, the wedding planner, who returned texts with a phone call and never met a cupcake tower she didn't like. Frances hired her when Holly had shown a distinct lack of enthusiasm for planning her own wedding. Holly wasn't in any hurry; they hadn't even set a date yet. But the parents were getting restless.

She and Brit had been engaged for six months, but they'd been betrothed for well beyond that as part of a murky business deal no one liked to talk about. Holly had grown up knowing someday she would marry Brit Anderson, the son of her father's partner. Like her, Brit had lived on the resort his whole life in an idyllic, sheltered childhood. Holly had never really given the betrothal much thought, but lately it had become impossible to push it from her mind, like a splinter beginning to fester.

In the hollow behind the cotoneasters, Holly dropped her head onto her knees as confusion and resentment flashed through her. Brit didn't look at her the way Darrin had looked at Nikki—and she didn't *want* him to look at her that way. He was a friend, nothing more, yet she was expected to make a lifetime commitment to him. Had her parents even considered what that meant? Their marriage wasn't the best, but at least it had been formed from love. Why didn't they want the same for her?

Her muscles were starting to cramp, and her secretary was probably wondering where she was. It wouldn't do any good to sit here moping. Holly unfolded herself with a sigh and crawled back through the tunnel toward the patch of sunshine at the end.

She poked her head out from around the swing in time to see a man pick up one of the shoes she'd left by the fountain.

"Hey!" Holly yelled.

Startled, he dropped the shoe, which bounced off the rock edge of the fountain and into the water with a splash.

Holly bounded to her feet and stalked across the grass. "Those are Jimmy Choos and they're *expensive*!" Glaring at him, she plunged her hand into the fountain's pool and pulled out the shoe, the soggy green suede now much darker than its original shade of celery.

"I'm sorry. I thought someone had gone off and forgotten their things." The man gestured to the grass, where Holly's other shoe sat alongside her soft leather briefcase. "What are you doing lurking in the bushes like some kind of goblin?" He dug in his pocket and offered her a folded white handkerchief.

"None of your business." Holly snatched the handkerchief and tried to sop up some of the water from the suede. "These are ruined."

"To be fair, only *that* one is ruined," the man said. "The other one seems fine."

She stared up into his eyes. They were dark, almost black, and were dancing with mirth under his heavy brows. He was several inches taller, broad-shouldered and big. She took in his clean-shaven, rather square jaw, and full lips set in a slightly cocky smile and felt the stirrings of butterflies in her stomach. His light brown hair curled over the edge of his collar and was adorably tousled.

Adorably? Wait … no.

"I'm very sorry for baptizing your shoe," he said, keeping the grin in place. "I'll reimburse you for it. Also, did you know you're bleeding?" He reached out and plucked the soggy handkerchief from her fingers and lightly brushed it over her cheek.

It must have been a scratch from the bushes, but Holly didn't feel anything beyond the zing of her nerves igniting at his touch. She jumped back.

"Whoa, settle down." He extended the handkerchief, showing her the small spot of red. "Bleeding … see?"

"Thanks." She took the handkerchief from him and pressed it to her cheek. "I'm Holly Clarke; who are you?"

Read more or buy The Rebellious One here.

Excerpt from *The Resilient Bride* by Lucy McConnell:

Liam Bernhard took a large bite of bienenstich and savored the vanilla flavor as the sweet pastry melted into his taste buds. "There's enough cream in this to choke a cow."

"You keep eating like this, and you will be a cow," countered his older brother, David.

Liam pointed at David's plate covered with large zwetschgenkuchen. "You're older than me. Your metabolism is slower."

David grunted. "I work out."

Liam grunted back. "Life's too short to live in a gym."

The zwetschgenkuchen went to the table and stayed on the square napkin like a forlorn and forgotten friend. Liam didn't mean to bring up his impending doom, but he just couldn't see the point of ignoring it like David wanted to. David, Liam's best friend and partner in crime, had been in a perpetual bad mood, and Liam was tired of living with Eeyore.

The last six months of revelry and dream-making darkened like the German sky above them. They'd skied, golfed, surfed, swum, biked, viewed priceless artwork, toured ancient ruins, dug for buried treasure, and even sailed the high seas. His more recent exploits had taken a domestic turn, and they'd sampled foods across the globe. Even now they occupied two chairs in a small German bakery with a full selection of the baker's wares spread before them. What did Liam care if he took one bite of everything?

"I've been thinking …" Liam trailed off, taking another large bite and chomping away like a kid at scout camp.

"Yeah?" David folded his arms.

"What this adventure needs is a woman's touch." Liam had David's full attention. "I'd like a warm body around once in a while."

"Exactly *what* do you have in mind?"

Liam reached into his shirt pocket and pulled out a business card he'd gotten from his trust fund manager.

"BMB?" David raised an eyebrow.

"Billionaire Marriage Brokers."

"You're out of your mind."

"A side effect from the tumor, I'm sure."

David glared at the table. "So what, you buy a wife? Isn't that human trafficking?"

"Hire. I would *hire* a wife uniquely chosen for me."

"Uniquely chosen by whom?"

Liam picked up a kreple. It looked like a donut. "Pamela Jones."

David licked icing off his thumb. "Is this prostitution? Do I need to call Mom?"

"Ha ha. No. There's no hanky-panky. It's in the contract." *Besides the fact that the drugs I'm on make* that *impossible* ... For that reason alone, he'd been happy to sign up for a business marriage — any marriage. The fact that Pamela could find him a wife who could also be his nurse was a benefit. David was a great brother and buddy, and Ella was an excellent personal secretary, but neither of them knew the first thing about medicine.

According to his doctor-issued time line, Liam had three months left. That was great on paper, but Liam suspected the doctor had been overly optimistic. He couldn't explain his premonition, just that he knew if he was going to find a bride, now was the time.

Liam wanted to be married before he died. He wanted to know what it was like to have someone to belong to, and if that meant going through Billionaire Marriage Brokers, then that's what he would do.

Read more or buy *The Resilient Bride* here.

Made in the USA
Columbia, SC
16 July 2023

20539658R00085